SNOW BUNTINGS.

WINTER SUNSHINE

BY

JOHN BURROUGHS

BOSTON AND NEW YORK
HOUGHTON, MIFFLIN AND COMPANY
The Riverside Press, Cambridge
1901

PREFATORY

The only part of my book I wish to preface is the last part, — the foreign sketches, — and it is not much matter about these, since, if they do not contain their own proof, I shall not attempt to supply it here.

I have been told that De Lolme, who wrote a notable book on the English Constitution, said that after he had been in England a few weeks, he fully made up his mind to write a book on that country; after he had lived there a year, he still thought of writing a book, but was not so certain about it, but that after a residence of ten years he abandoned his first design altogether. Instead of furnishing an argument against writing out one's first impressions of a country, I think the experience of the Frenchman shows the importance of doing it at once. The sensations of the first day are what we want, — the first flush of the traveler's thought and feeling, before his perception and sensibilities become cloyed or blunted, or before he in any way becomes a part of that which he would observe and describe. Then the American in England is just enough at home to enable him to discriminate subtle shades and differ-

ences at first sight which might escape a traveler of another and antagonistic race. He has brought with him, but little modified or impaired, his whole inheritance of English ideas and predilections, and much of what he sees affects him like a memory. It is his own past, his ante-natal life, and his long-buried ancestors look through his eyes and perceive with his sense.

I have attempted only the surface, and to express my own first day's uncloyed and unalloyed satisfaction. Of course I have put these things through my own processes and given them my own coloring (as who would not), and if other travelers do not find what I did, it is no fault of mine; or if the " Britishers " do not deserve all the pleasant things I say of them, why then so much the worse for them.

In fact, if it shall appear that I have treated this part in the same spirit that I have the themes in the other chapters, reporting only such things as impressed me and stuck to me and tasted good, I shall be satisfied.

Esopus-ON-HuDSON, November, 1875.

CONTENTS

WINTER SUNSHINE

WINTEK SUNSHINE

A N American resident in England is reported as saying that the English have an atmosphere but no climate. The reverse of this remark would apply pretty accurately to our own case. We certainly have a climate, a two-edged one that cuts both ways, threatening us with sun-stroke on the one hand and with frost-stroke on the other; but we have no atmosphere to speak of in New York and New England, except now and then during the dog-days, or the fitful and uncertain Indian Summer. An atmosphere, the quality of tone and mellowness in the near distance, is the product of a more humid climate. Hence, as we go south from New York, the atmospheric effects become more rich and varied, until on reaching the Potomac you find an atmosphere as well as a climate. The latter is still on the vehement American scale, full of sharp and violent changes and contrasts, baking and blistering in summer, and nipping and blighting in winter, but the spaces are not so purged and bare;

the horizon wall does not so often have the appearance of having just been washed and scrubbed down. There is more depth and visibility to the open air, a stronger infusion of the Indian Summer element throughout the year, than is found farther north. The days are softer and more brooding, and the nights more enchanting. It is here that Walt Whitman saw the full moon

"Pour down Night's nimbus floods," as any one may see her, during her full, from October to May. There is more haze and vapor in the atmosphere during that period, and every particle seems to collect and hold the pure radiance until the world swims with the lunar outpouring. Is not the full moon always on the side of fair weather ? I think it is Sir William Herschel who says her influence tends to dispel the clouds. Certain it is her beauty is seldom lost or even veiled in this southern or semi-southern clime.

It is here also the poet speaks of the

" Floods of the 3'ellow gold of the gorgeous, Indolent sinking sun, burning, expanding the air,"

a description that would not apply with the same force farther north, where the air seems thinner and less capable of absorbing and holding the sunlight. Indeed, the opulence and splendor of our climate, at least the climate of our Atlantic seaboard, cannot be fully appreciated by the dweller north of the thirty-ninth parallel. It seemed as if I had never seen but a second-rate article of sunlight or moonlight until I had taken up my abode in the National

Capital. It may be, perhaps, because we have such splendid specimens of both at that period of the year when one values such things highest, namely, in the fall and winter and early spring. Sunlight is good any time, but a bright, evenly tempered day is certainly more engrossing to the attention in winter than in summer, and such days seem the rule, and not the exception, in the Washington winter. The deep snows keep to the north, the heavy rains to the south, leaving a blue space central over the border States. And there is not one of the winter months but wears this blue zone as a girdle.

I am not thinking especially of the Indian Summer, that charming but uncertain second youth of the New England year, but of regularly recurring lucid intervals in the weather system of the Virginia fall and winter, when the best our climate is capable of stands revealed, — southern days with northern blood in their veins, exhilarating, elastic, full of action, the hyperborean oxygen of the North tempered by the dazzling sun of the South, a little bitter in winter to all travelers but the pedestrian, — to him sweet and warming, — but in autumn a vintage that intoxicates all lovers of the open air.

It is impossible not to dilate and expand under such skies. One breathes deeply and steps proudly, and if he have any of the eagle nature in him it comes to the surface then. There is a sense of altitude about these dazzling November and December days, of mountain tops and pure ether. The

earth in passing through the fire of summer seems to have lost all its dross, and life all its impediments.

But what does not the dweller in the National Capital endure in reaching these days! Think of the agonies of the heated term, the ragings of the dog-star, the purgatory of heat and dust, of baking, blistering pavements, of cracked and powdered fields, of dead, stifling night air, from which every tonic and antiseptic quality seems eliminated, leaving a residuum of sultry malaria and all-diffusing privy and sewer gases, that lasts from the first of July to near the middle of September! But when October is reached, the memory of these things is afar off", and the glory of the days is a perpetual surprise.

I sally out in the morning with the ostensible purpose of gathering chestnuts, or autumn leaves, or persimmons, or exploring some run or branch. It is, say, the last of October or the first of November. The air is not balmy, but tart and pungent, like the flavor of the red-cheeked apples by the roadside. In the sky not a cloud, not a speck; a vast dome of blue ether lightly suspended above the world. The woods are heaped with color like a painter's palette, —great splashes of red and orange and gold. The ponds and streams bear upon their bosoms leaves of all tints, from the deep maroon of the oak to the pale yellow of the chestnut. In the glens and nooks it is so still that the chirp of a solitary cricket is noticeable. The red berries of

the dogwood and spice-bush and other shrubs shina in the sun like rubies and coral. The crows fly high above the earth, as they do only on such days, forms of ebony floating across the azure, and the buzzards look like kingly birds, sailing round and round.

Or it may be later in the season, well into December. The days are equally bright, but a little more rugged. The mornings are ushered in by an immense spectrum thrown upon the eastern sky. A broad bar of red and orange lies along the low horizon, surmounted by an expanse of color in which green struggles with yellow and blue with green half the way to the zenith. By and by the red and orange spread upward and grow dim, the spectrum fades, and the sky becomes suffused with yellow white light, and in a moment the fiery scintillations of the sun begin to break across the Maryland hills. Then before long the mists and vapors uprise like the breath of a giant army, and for an hour or two one is reminded of a November morning in England. But by mid-forenoon the only trace of the obscurity that remains is a slight haze, and the day is indeed a summons and a challenge to come forth. If the October days were a cordial like the sub-acids of fruit, these are a tonic like the wine of iron. Drink deep, or be careful how you taste this December vintage. The first sip may chill, but a full draught warms and invigorates. No loitering by the brooks or in the woods now, but spirited, rugged walking along the public high* way. The sunbeams are welcome now. They seem like pure electricity, —-'like friendly and recuperating lightning. Are we led to think electricity abounds only in summer when we see in the storm-clouds, as it were, the veins and ore-beds of it? I imagine it is equally abundant in winter, and more equable and better tempered. Who ever breasted a snowstorm without being excited and exhilarated, as if this meteor had come charged with latent aurorae of the North, as doubtless it has 1 It is like being pelted with sparks from a battery. Behold the frostwork on the pane, — the wild, fantastic lim-nings and etchings! can there be any doubt but this subtle agent has been here 1 Where is it not ? It is the life of the crystal, the architect of the flake, the fire of the frost, the soul of the sunbeam. This crisp winter air is full of it. When I come in at night after an all-day tramp I am charged like a Leyden jar; my hair crackles and snaps beneath the comb like a cat's back, and a strange, new glow diffuses itself through my system.

It is a spur that one feels at this season more than at any other. How nimbly you step forth! The woods roar, the waters shine, and the hills look invitingly near. You do not miss the flowers and the songsters, or wish the trees or the fields any different, or the heavens any nearer. Every object pleases. A rail fence, running athwart the hills, now in sunshine and now in shadow, — how the eye lingers upon it! Or the straight, light-gray trunks of the trees, where the woods have recently been

laid open by a road or a clearing, — how curious they look, and as if surprised in undress! Next year they will begin to shoot out branches and make themselves a screen. Or the farm scenes, —the winter barnyards littered with husks and straw, the rough-coated horses, the cattle sunning themselves or walking down to the spring to drink, the domestic fowls moving about, — there is a touch of sweet, homely life in these things that the winter sun enhances and brings out. Every sign of life is welcome at this season. I love to hear dogs bark, hens cackle, and boys shout; one has no privacy with Nature now, and does not wish to seek her in nooks and hidden ways. She is not at home if he goes there; her house is shut up and her hearth cold; only the sun and sky, and perchance the waters, wear the old look, and to-day we will make love to them, and they shall abundantly return it.

Even the crows and the buzzards draw the eye fondly. The National Capital is a great place for buzzards, and I make the remark in no double or allegorical sense either, for the buzzards I mean are black and harmless as doves, though perhaps hardly dovelike in their tastes. My vulture is also a bird of leisure, and sails through the ether on long flexible pinions, as if that was the one delight of his life. Some birds have wings, others have "pinions." The buzzard enjoys this latter distinction. There is something in the sound of the word that suggests that easy, dignified, undulatory movement. He does not propel himself along by sheer force of

WINTER SUNSHINE

muscle, after the plebeian fashion of the crow for instance, but progresses by a kind of royal indirection that puzzles the eye. Even on a windy winter day he rides the vast aerial billows as placidly as ever, rising and falling as he comes up toward you, carving his way through the resisting currents by a slight oscillation to the right and left, but never once beating the air openly.

This superabundance of wing power is very unequally distributed among the feathered races, the hawks and vultures having by far the greater share of it. They cannot command the most speed, but their apparatus seems the most delicate and consummate. Apparently a fine play of muscle, a subtle shifting of the power along the outstretched wings, a perpetual loss and a perpetual recovery of the equipoise, sustains them and bears them along. With them flying is a luxury, a fine art, not merely a quicker and safer means of transit from one point to another, but a gift so free and spontaneous that work becomes leisure and movement rest. They are not so much going somewhere, from this perch to that, as they are abandoning themselves to the mere pleasure of riding upon the air.

And it is beneath such grace and high-bred leisure that Nature hides in her creatures the occupation of scavenger and carrion-eater!

But the worst thing about the buzzard is his silence. The crow caws, the hawk screams, the eagle barks, but the buzzard says not a word. So far as I have observed, he has no vocal powers what-

ever. Nature dare not trust him to speak. In his case she preserves a discreet silence.

The crow may not have the sweet voice which the fox in his flattery attributed to him, but he has a good, strong, native speech nevertheless. How much character there is in it! How much thrift and independence! Of course his plumage is firm, his color decided, his wit quick. He understands you at once and tells you so; so does the hawk by his scornful, defiant ivJiir-r-r-r. Hardy, happy outlaws, the crows, how I love them! Alert, social, republican, always able to look out for himself, not afraid of the cold and the snow, fishing when flesh is scarce, and stealing when other resources fail, the crow is a character I would not willingly miss from the landscape. I love to see his track in the snow or the mud, and his graceful pedestrianism about the brown fields.

He is no interloper, but has the air and manner of being thoroughly at home, and in rightful possession of the land. He is no sentimentalist like some of the plaining, disconsolate song-birds, but apparently is always in good health and good spirits. No matter who is sick, or dejected, or unsatisfied, or what the weather is, or what the price of corn, the crow is well and finds life sweet. He is the dusky embodiment of worldly wisdom and prudence. Then he is one of Nature's self-appointed constables and greatly magnifies his oflice. He would fain arrest every hawk or owl or grimalkin that ventures abroad. I have known a posse of them to beset the

fox and cry " Thief! " till Keynard hid himself for shame. Do I say the fox flattered the crow when he told him he had a sweet voice ? Yet one of the most musical sounds in nature proceeds from the crow. All the crow tribe, from the blue jay up, are capable of certain low ventriloquial notes that have peculiar cadence and charm. I often hear the crow indulging in his in winter, and am reminded of the sound of the dulcimer. The bird stretches up and exerts himself like a cock in the act of crowing and gives forth a peculiarly clear, vitreous sound that is sure to arrest and reward your attention. This is no doubt the song the fox begged to be favored with, as in delivering it the crow must inevitably let drop the piece of meat.

The crow in his purity, I believe, is seen and heard only in the North. Before you reach the Potomac there is an infusion of a weaker element, the fish crow, whose helpless feminine call contrasts strongly with the hearty masculine caw of the original Simon.

In passing from crows to colored men, I hope I am not guilty of any disrespect toward the latter. In my walks about Washington, both winter and summer, colored men are about the only pedestrians I meet; and I meet them everywhere, in the fields and in the woods and in the public road, swinging along with that peculiar, rambling, elastic gait, taking advantage of the short cuts and threading the country with paths and byways. I doubt if the colored man can compete with his white brother aa

a walker; his foot is too flat and the calves of his legs too small, but he is certainly the most picturesque traveler to be seen on the road. He bends his knees more than the white man, and oscillates more to and fro, or from side to side. The imaginary line which his head describes is full of deep and long undulations. Even the boys and young men sway as if bearing a burden.

Along the fences and by the woods I come upon their snares, dead-falls, and rude box-traps. The freedman is a successful trapper and hunter, and has by nature an insight into these things. I frequently see him in market or on his way thither with a tame 'possum clinging timidly to his shoulders, or a young coon or fox led by a chain. Indeed, the colored man behaves precisely like the rude unsophisticated peasant that he is, and there is fully as much virtue in him, using the word in its true sense, as in the white peasant; indeed, much more than in the poor whites who grew up by his side; while there is often a benignity and a depth of human experience and sympathy about some of these dark faces that comes home to one like the best one sees in art or reads in books.

One touch of nature makes all the world akin, and there is certainly a touch of nature about the colored man; indeed, I had almost said, of Anglo-Saxon nature. They have the quaintness and homeliness of the simple English stock. I seem to see my grandfather and grandmother in the ways and doings of these old "uncles" and "aunties;" in-deed, the lesson comes nearer home than even that, for I seem to see myself in them, and, what is more, I see that they see themselves in me, and that neither party has much to boast of.

The negro is a plastic human creature, and is thoroughly domesticated and thoroughly anglicized. The same cannot be said of the Indian for instance, between us and whom there can never exist any fellowship, any community of feeling or interest; or is there any doubt but the Chinaman will always remain to us the same impenetrable mystery he has been from the first ?

But there is no mystery about the negro, and he touches the Anglo-Saxon at more points than the latter is always willing to own, taking as kindly and naturally to all his customs and usages, yea, to all his prejudices and superstitions, as if to the manor born. The colored population in very many respects occupies the same position as that occupied by our rural populations a generation or two ago, seeing signs and wonders, haunted by the fear of ghosts and hobgoblins, believing in witchcraft, charms, the evil eye, etc. In religious matters, also, they are on the same level, and about the only genuine shouting Methodists that remain are to be found in the colored churches. Indeed, I fear the negro tries to ignore or forget himself as far as possible, and that he would deem it felicity enough to play second fiddle to the white man all his days. He liked his master, but he likes the Yankee better, not because he regards him as his deliverer, but mainly because the two-handed thrift of the Northerner, his varied and wonderful ability, completely captivates the imagination of the black man, just learning to shift for himself.

How far he has caught or is capable of being imbued with the Yankee spirit of enterprise and industry, remains to be seen. In some things he has already shown himself an apt scholar. I notice, for instance, he is about as industrious an office-seeker as the most patriotic among us, and that he learns with amazing ease and rapidity all the arts and wiles of the politicians. He is versed in parades, mass meetings, caucuses, and will soon shine on the stump. I observe, also, that he is not far behind us in the observance of the fashions, and that he is as good a church-goer, theatre-goer, and pleasure-seeker generally, as his means will allow.

As a bootblack or newsboy, he is an adept in all the tricks of the trade; and as a fast young man about town among his kind, he is worthy his white prototype: the swagger, the impertinent look, the coarse remark, the loud laugh, are all in the best style. As a lounger and starer also, on the street corners of a Sunday afternoon, he has taken his degree.

On the other hand, I know cases among our colored brethren, plenty of them, of conscientious and well-directed effort and industry in the worthiest fields, in agriculture, in trade, in the mechanic arts, that show the colored man has in him all the best rudiments of a citizen of the States.

Lest my winter sunshine appear to have too many dark rays in it, — buzzards, crows, and colored men, — I hasten to add the brown and neutral tints, and may be a red ray can be extracted from some of these hard, smooth, sharp-gritted roads that radiate from the National Capital. Leading out of Washington there are several good roads that invite the pedestrian. There is the road that leads west or northwest from Georgetown, the Tenallytown road, the very sight of which, on a sharp, lustrous winter Sunday, makes the feet tingle. Wliere it cuts through a hill or high knoll, it is so red it fairly glows in the sunlight. I '11 warrant you will kindle, and your own color will mount, if you resign yourself to it. It will conduct you to the wild and rocky scenery of the upper Potomac, to Great Falls, and on to Harper's Ferry, if your courage holds out. Then there is the road that leads north over Meridian Hill, across Piny Branch, and on through the wood of Crystal Springs to Fort Stevens, and so into Maryland. This is the proper route for an excursion in the spring to gather wild flowers, or in the fall for a nutting expedition, as it lays open some noble woods and a great variety of charming scenery; or for a musing moonlight saunter, say in December, when the Enchantress has folded and folded the world in her web, it is by all means the course to take. Your staff rings on the hard ground; the road, a misty white belt, gleams and vanishes before you; the woods are cavernous and still; the fields lie in a lunar trance, and you will

yourself return fairly mesmerized by the beauty of the scene.

Or you can bend your steps eastward over the Eastern Branch, up Good Hope Hill, and on till you strike the Marlborough pike, as a trio of us did that cold February Sunday we walked from Washington to Pumpkintown and back.

A short sketch of this pilgrimage is a fair sample of these winter walks.

The delight I experienced in making this new acquisition to my geography was of itself sufficient to atone for any aches or weariness I may have felt. The mere fact that one may walk from Washington to Pumpkintown was a discovery I had been all these years in making. I had walked to Sligo, and to the Northwest Branch, and had made the Falls of the Potomac in a circuitous route of ten miles, coming suddenly upon the river in one of its wildest passes; but I little dreamed all the while that there, in a wrinkle (or shall I say furrow ?) of the Maryland hills, almost visible from the outlook of the bronze squaw on the dome of the Capitol, and just around the head of Oxen E,un, lay Pumpkintown.

The day was cold but the sun was bright, and the foot took hold of those hard, dry, gritty Maryland roads with the keenest relish. How the leaves of the laurel glistened! The distant oak woods Buggested gray-blue smoke, while the recesses of the pines looked like the lair of Night. Beyond the District limits we struck the Marlborough pike, which, round and hard and white, held squarely to

the east and was visible a mile ahead. Its friction brought up the temperature amazingly and spurred the pedestrians into their best time. As I trudged along, Thoreau's lines came naturally to mind: —

" When the spring stirs my blood With the instinct of travel, I can get enough gravel On the old Marlborough road."

Cold as the day was (many degrees below freezing), I heard and saw bluebirds, and as we passed along every sheltered tangle and overgrown field or lane swarmed with snowbirds and sparrows, — the latter mainly Canada or tree sparrows, with a sprinkling of the song, and, maybe, one or two other varieties. The birds are all social and gregarious in winter, and seem drawn together by common instinct. Where you find one, you will not only find others of the same kind, but also several different kinds. The regular winter residents go in little bands, like a well-organized pioneer corps, — the jays and woodpeckers in advance, doing the heavier work; the nuthatches next, more lightly armed; and the creepers and kinglets, with their slender beaks and microscopic eyes, last of all. ^

Now and then, among the gray and brown tints, there was a dash of scarlet, — the cardinal grosbeak, whose presence was sufficient to enliven any scene. In the leafless trees, as a ray of sunshine fell upon him, he was visible a long way off, glowing like a

1 It seems to me this is a borrowed observation, but I do not know whom to credit it to.

crimson spar, — the only bit of color in the whole landscape.

Maryland is here rather a level, nnpicturesque country, — the gaze of the traveler bounded, at no great distance, by oak woods, with here and there a dark line of pine. We saw few travelers, passed a ragged squad or two of colored boys and girls, and met some colored women on their way to or from church, perhaps. Never ask a colored person — at least the crude, rustic specimens — any question that involves a memory of names, or any arbitrary signs; you will rarely get a satisfactory answer. If you could speak to them in their own dialect, or touch the right spring in their minds, you would, no doubt, get the desired information. They are as local in their notions and habits as the animals, and go on much the same principles, as no doubt we all do, more or less. I saw a colored boy come into a public office one day, and ask to see a man with red hair; the name was utterly gone from him. The man had red whiskers, which was as near as he had come to the mark. Ask your washerwoman what street she lives on, or where such a one has moved to, and the chances are that she cannot tell you, except that it is a "right smart distance" this way or that, or near Mr. So-and-so, or by such and such a place, describing some local feature. I love to amuse myself, when walking through the market, by asking the old aunties, and the young aunties, too, the names of their various "yarbs." It seems as if they must trip on the simplest names. Blood-

root they generally call "grubroot;" trailing arbutus goes by the names of "troling" arbutus, "training arbuty-flower," and ground "ivory;" in Virginia they call woodchucks "moonacks."

On entering Pumpkintown — a cluster of five or six small, whitewashed blockhouses, toeing squarely on the highway — the only inhabitant we saw was a small boy, who was as frank and simple as if he had lived on pumpkins and marrow squashes all his days.

Half a mile farther on, we turned to the right into a characteristic Southern road, — a Avay entirely unkempt, and wandering free as the wind; now fading out into a broad field; now contracting into a narrow track between hedges; anon roaming with delightful abandon through swamps and woods, asking no leave and keeping no bounds. About two o'clock we stopped in an opening in a pine wood and ate our lunch. We had the good fortune to hit upon a charming place. A wood-chopper had been there, and let in the sunlight full and strong; and the white chips, the newly-piled wood, and the mounds of green boughs, were welcome features, and helped also to keep ofi" the wind that would creep through under the pines. The ground was soft and dry, with a carpet an inch thick of pine-needles, and with a fire, less for warmth than to make the picture complete, we ate our bread and beans with the keenest satisfaction, and with a relish that only the open air can give.

A fire, of course, — an encampment in the woods

at this season without a fire would be like leaving Hamlet out of the play. A smoke is your standard, yovir flag; it defines and locates your camp at once; you are an interloper until you have made a fire; then you take possession; then the trees and rocks seem to look upon you more kindly, and you look more kindly upon them. As one opens his budget, so he opens his heart by a fire. Already something has gone out from you, and comes back as a faint reminiscence and home feeling in the air and place. One looks out upon the crow or the buzzard that sails by as from his own fireside. It is not I that am a wanderer and a stranger now; it is the crow and the buzzard. The chickadees were silent at first, but now they approach by little journeys, as if to make our acquaintance. The nuthatches, also, cry " Yank! yank!" in no inhospitable tones; and those purple finches there in the cedars, — are they not stealing our berries ?

How one lingers about a fire under such circumstances, loath to leave it, poking up the sticks, throwing in the burnt ends, adding another branch and yet another, and looking back as he turns to go to catch one more glimpse of the smoke going up through the trees! I reckon it is some remnant of the primitive man, which we all carry about with us. He has not yet forgotten his wild, free life, his arboreal habitations, and the sweet-bitter times he had in those long-gone ages. With me, he wakes up directly at the smell of smoke, of burning branches in the open air; and all his old love of

fire and dependence upon it, in the camp or the cave, comes freshly to mind.

On resuming our march, we filed off along a charming wood-path,— a regular little tunnel through the dense pines, carpeted with silence, and allowing us to look nearly the whole length of it through its soft green twilight out into the open sunshine of the fields beyond. A pine wood in Maryland or in Virginia is quite a different thing from a pine wood in Maine or Minnesota, — the difference, in fact, between yellow pine and white. The former, as it grows hereabout, is short and scrubby, with branches nearly to the ground, and looks like the dwindling remnant of a greater race.

Beyond the woods, the path led us by a colored man's habitation,—a little, low frame house, on a knoll, surrounded by the quaint devices and rude makeshifts of these quaint and rude people. A few poles stuck in the ground, clapboarded with cedar-boughs and cornstalks, and supporting a roof of the same, gave shelter to a rickety one-horse wagon and some farm implements. Near this there was a large, compact tent, made entirely of cornstalks, ^yith, for door, a bundle of the same, in the dry, warm, nest-like interior of which the husking of the corn crop seemed to have taken place. A few rods farther on, we passed through another humble dooryard, musical with dogs and dusky with children. We.crossed here the outlying fields of a large, thrifty, well-kept-looking farm with a showy, highly ornamental frame house in the centre.

There was even a park with deer, and among the gayly painted outbuildings I noticed a fancy dovecote, with an immense flock of doves circling above it; some whiskey-dealer from the city, we were told, trying to take the poison out of his money by agriculture.

We next passed through some woods, when we emerged into a broad, sunlit, fertile-looking valley, called Oxen Run. We stooped down and drank of its clear white-pebbled stream, in the veritable spot, I suspect, where the oxen do. There were clouds of birds here on the warm slopes, with the usual sprinkling along the bushy margin of the stream of scarlet grosbeaks. The valley of Oxen Kun has many good-looking farms, with old picturesque houses, and loose rambling barns, such as artists love to put into pictures.

But it is a little awkward to go cast. It ahvays seems left-handed. I think this is the feeling of all walkers, and that Thoreau's experience in this respect was not singular. The great magnet is the sun, and we follow him. I notice that people lost in the woods work to the westward. When one comes out of his house and asks himself, "Which way shall I walk 1 " and looks up and down and around for a sign or a token, does he not nine times out of ten turn to the west? He inclines this way as surely as the willow wand bends toward the water. There is something more genial and friendly in this direction.

Occasionally in winter I experience a southern inclination, and cross Long Bridge and rendezvous for the day in some old earthwork on the Virginia hills. The roads are not so inviting in this direction, but the line of old forts with rabbits burrowing in the bomb-proofs, and a magazine, or officers' quarters turned into a cow stable by colored squatters, form an interesting feature. But, whichever way I go, I am glad I came. All roads lead up to the Jerusalem the walker seeks. There is everywhere the vigorous and masculine winter air, and the impalpable sustenance the mind draws from all natural forms.

THE EXHILAEATIONS OF THE KOAD

Afoot and light-hearted I take to the open road.

Walt Whitman.

OCCASIONALLY on the sidewalk, amid the dapper, swiftly-moving, high-heeled boots and gaiters, I catch a glimpse of the naked human foot. Nimbly it scuffs along, the toes spread, the sides flatten, the heel protrudes; it grasps the curbing, or bends to the form of the uneven surfaces, — a thing sensuous and alive, that seems to take cognizance of whatever it touches or passes. How primitive and uncivil it looks in such company, — a real barbarian in the parlor! We are so unused to the human anatomy, to simple, unadorned nature, that it looks a little repulsive; but it is beautiful for all that. Though it be a black foot and an unwashed foot, it shall be exalted. It is a thing of life amid leather, a free spirit amid cramped, a wild bird amid caged, an athlete amid consumptives. It is the symbol of my order, the Order of Walkers. That unhampered, vitally playing piece of anatomy is the type of the pedestrian, man returned to first principles, in direct contact and intercourse with the earth and the elements, his faculties unsheathed.

his mind plastic, his body toughened, his heart light, his soul dilated; while those cramped and distorted members in the calf and kid are the unfortunate wretches doomed to carriages and cushions.

I am not going to advocate the disuse of boots and shoes, or the abandoning of the improved modes of travel; but I am going to brag as lustily as I can on behalf of the pedestrian, and show how all the shining angels second and accompany the man who goes afoot, while all the dark spirits are ever looking out for a chance to ride.

When I see the discomforts that able-bodied American men will put up with rather than go a mile or half a mile on foot, the abuses they Avill tolerate and encourage, crowding the street car on a little fall in the temperature or the appearance of an inch or two of snow, packing up to overflowing, dangling to the straps, treading on each other's toes, breathing each other's breaths, crushing the women and children, hanging by tooth and nail to a square inch of the platform, imperiling their limbs and killing the horses, — I think the commonest tramp in the street has good reason to felicitate himself on his rare privilege of going afoot. Indeed, a race that neglects or despises this primitive gift, that fears the touch of the soil, that has no footpaths, no community of ownership in the land which they imply, that warns off" the walker as a trespasser, that knows no way but the highway, the carriage-way, that forgets the stile, the footbridge, that even ignores the rights of the pedes-

trian in the public road, providing no escape for him but in the ditch or up the bank, is in a fair way to far more serious degeneracy.

Shakespeare makes the chief qualification of the walker a merry heart: —

" Jog on, jog on, the footpath way,

And merrily hent the stile-a;

A merry heart goes all the clay, -

Your sad tires in a mile-a."

The human body is a steed that goes freest and longest under a light rider, and the lightest of all riders is a cheerful heart. Your sad, or morose, or embittered, or preoccupied heart settles heavily into the saddle, and the poor beast, the body, breaks down the first mile. Indeed, the heaviest thing in the world is a heavy heart. Next to that, the most burdensome to the walker is a heart not in perfect sympathy and accord with the body, — a reluctant or unwilling heart. The horse and rider must not only both be willing to go the same way, but the rider must lead the way and infuse his own lightness and eagerness into the steed. Herein is no doubt our trouble, and one reason of the decay of the noble art in this country. We are unwilling walkers. We are not innocent and simple-hearted enough to enjoy a walk. We have fallen from that state of grace which capacity to enjoy a walk implies. It cannot be said that as a people we are so positively sad, or morose, or melancholic as that we are vacant of that sportiveness and surplusage of animal spirits that characterized our ancestors, and

that springs from full and harmonious life, —a sound heart in accord with a sound body. A man must invest himself near at hand and in common things, and be content with a steady and moderate return, if he would know the blessedness of a cheerful heart and the sweetness of a walk over the round earth. This is a lesson the American has yet to learn, — capability of amusement on a low key. He expects rapid and extraordinary returns. He would make the very elemental laws pay usury. He has nothing to invest in a walk; it is too slow, too cheap. We crave the astonishing, the exciting, the far away, and do not know the highways of the gods when we see them, — always a sign of the decay of the faith and simplicity of man.

If I say to my neighbor, " Come with me, I have great wonders to show you," he pricks up his ears and comes forthwith; but when I take him on the hills under the full blaze of the sun, or along the country road, our footsteps lighted by the moon and stars, and say to him, "Behold, these are the wonders, these are the circuits of the gods, this we now tread is a morning star," he feels defrauded, and as if I had played him a trick. And yet nothing less than dilatation and enthusiasm like this is the badge of the master walker.

If we are not sad, we are careworn, hurried, discontented, mortgaging the present for the promise of the future. If we take a walk, it is as we take a prescription, with about the same relish and with about tlie same purpose; and the more the

iatigue the greater our faith in the virtue of the medicine.

Of these gleesome saunters over the hills in spring, or those sallies of the body in winter, those excursions into space when the foot strikes fire at every step, when the air tastes like a new and finer mixture, when we accumulate force and gladness as we go along, when the sight of objects by the roadside and of the fields and woods pleases more than pictures or than all the art in the world, — those ten or twelve mile dashes that are but the wit and effluence of the corporeal powers, —of such diversion and open road entertainment, I say, most of us know very little.

I notice with astonishment that at our fashionable watering-places nobody walks; that, of all those vast crowds of health-seekers and lovers of country air, you can never catch one in the fields or woods, or guilty of trudging along the country road with dust on his shoes and sun-tan on his hands and face. The sole amusement seems to be to eat and dress and sit about the hotels and glare at each other. The men look bored, the women look tired, and all seem to sigh, "O Lord! what shall we do to be happy and not be vulgar ?" Quite different from our British cousins across the water, who have plenty of amusement and hilarity, spending most of the time at their watering-places in the open air, strolling, picnicking, boating, climbing, briskly walking, apparently with little fear of sun-tan or of compromising their "gentility."

It is indeed astonishing with what ease and hilarity the English walk. To an American it seems a kind of infatuation. When Dickens was in this country, I imagine the aspirants to the honor of a walk with him were not numerous. In a pedestrian tour of England by an American, I read that, " after breakfast with the Independent minister, he walked with us for six miles out of town upon our road. Three little boys and girls, the youngest six years old, also accompanied us. They were romping and rambling about all the while, and their morning walk must have been as much as fifteen miles; but they thought nothing of it, and when we parted were apparently as fresh as when they started, and very loath to return."

I fear, also, the American is becoming disqualified for the manly art of walking by a falling off in the size of his foot. He cherishes and cultivates this part of his anatomy, and apparently thinks his taste and good breeding are to be inferred from its diminutive size. A small, trim foot, well booted or gaitered, is the national vanity. How we stare at the big feet of foreigners, and wonder what may be the price of leather in those countries, and where all the aristocratic blood is, that these plebeian extremities so predominate! If we were admitted to the confidences of the shoemaker to Her Majesty or to His Koyal Highness, no doubt we would modify our views upon this latter point, for a truly large and royal nature is never stunted in the extremities; a little foot never yet supported a great character.

It is said that Englishmen when they first come to this country are for some time under the impression that American women all have deformed feet, they are so coy of them and so studiously careful to keep them hid. That there is an astonishing difference between the women of the two countries in this respect, every traveler can testify; and that there is a difference equally astonishing between the pedestrian habits and capabilities of the rival sisters, is also certain.

The English pedestrian, no doubt, has the advantage of us in the matter of climate; for, notwithstanding the traditional gloom and moroseness of English skies, they have in that country none of those relaxing, sinking, enervating days, of which we have so many here, and which seem especially trying to the female constitution, — days which withdraw all support from the back and loins, and render walking of all things burdensome. Theirs is a climate of which it has been said that " it invites men abroad more days in the year and more hours in the day than that of any other country."

Then their land is threaded with paths which invite the walker, and which are scarcely less important than the highways. I heard of a surly nobleman near London who took it into his head to close a footpath that passed through his estate near his house, and open another one a little farther off. The pedestrians objected; the matter got into the courts, and after protracted litigation the aristocrat was beaten. The path could not be closed or

moved. The memory of man ran not to the time when there was not a footpath there, and every pedestrian should have the right of way there still.

I remember the pleasure I had in the path that connects Stratford-on-A von with Shottery, Shakespeare's path when he went courting Anne Hathaway. By the king's highway the distance is some farther, so there is a well-worn path along the hedgerows and through the meadows and turnip patches. The traveler in it has the privilege of crossing the railroad track, an unusual privilege in England, and one denied to the lord in his carriage, who must either go over or under it. (It is a privilege, is it not, to be allowed the forbidden, even if it be the privilege of being run over by the engine?) In strolling over the South Downs, too, I was delighted to find that where the hill was steepest some benefactor of the order of walkers had made notches in the sward, so that the foot could bite the better and firmer; the path became a kind of stairway, which I have no doubt the plowman respected.

When you see an English country church withdrawn, secluded, out of the reach of wheels, standing amid grassy graves and surrounded by noble trees, approached by paths and shaded lanes, you appreciate more than ever this beautiful habit of the people. Only a race that knows how to use its feet, and holds footpaths sacred, could put such a charm of privacy and humility into such a structure. I think I should be tempted to go to church myself if I saw all my neighbors starting off across the

fields or along paths that led to such charmed spots, and was sure I would not be jostled or run over by the rival chariots of the worshipers at the temple doors. I think this is what ails our religion; humility and devoutness of heart leave one when he lays by his walking shoes and walking clothes, and sets out for church drawn by something.

Indeed, I think it would be tantamount to an astonishing revival of religion if the people would all walk to church on Sunday and walk home again. Think how the stones would preach to them by the wayside; how their benumbed minds would warm up beneath the friction of the gravel; how their vain and foolish thoughts, their desponding thoughts, their besetting demons of one kind and another, would drop behind them, unable to keep up or to endure the fresh air! They would walk away from their ennui, their worldly cares, their uncharitable-ness, their pride of dress; for these devils always want to ride, while the simple virtues are never so happy as when on foot. Let us walk by all means; but if we will ride, get an ass.

Then the English claim that they are a more hearty and robust people than we are. It is certain they are a plainer people, have plainer tastes, dress plainer, build plainer, speak plainer, keep closer to facts, wear broader shoes and coarser clothes, place a lower estimate on themselves, etc., — all of which traits favor pedestrian habits. The English grandee is not confined to his carriage; but if the American aristocrat leaves his, he is ruined. Oh the weari-

ness, the emptiness, the plotting, the seeking rest and finding none, that goes by in the carriages! while your pedestrian is always cheerful, alert, refreshed, with his heart in his hand and his hand free to all. He looks down upon nobody; he is on the common level. His pores are all open, his circulation is active, his digestion good. His heart is not cold, nor his faculties asleep. He is the only real traveler; he alone tastes the "gay, fresh sentiment of the road." He is not isolated, but one with things, with the farms and industries on either hand. The vital, universal currents play through him. He knows the ground is alive; he feels the pulses of the wind, and reads the mute language of things. His sympathies are all aroused; his senses are continually reporting messages to his mind. Wind, frost, rain, heat, cold, are something to him. He is not merely a spectator of the panorama of nature, but a participator in it. He experiences the country he passes through, — tastes it, feels it, absorbs it; the traveler in his fine carriage sees it merely. This gives the fresh charm to that class of books that may be called "Views Afoot," and to the narratives of hunters, naturalists, exploring parties, etc. The walker does not need a large territory. When you get into a. railway car you want a continent, the man in his carriage requires a township; but a walker like Thoreau finds as much and more along the shores of Walden Pond. The former, as it were, has merely time to glance at the headings of the chapters, while the latter need not

miss a line, and Thoreau reads between the lines. Then the walker has the privilege of the fields, the woods, the hills, the byways. The apples by the roadside are for him, and the berries, and the spring of water, and the friendly shelter; and if the weather is cold, he eats the frost grapes and the persimmons, or even the white-meated turnip, snatched from the field he passed through, with incredible relish.

Afoot and in the open road, one has a fair start in life at last. There is no hindrance now. Let him put his best foot forward. He is on the broadest human plane. This is on the level of all the great laws and heroic deeds. From this platform he is eligible to any good fortune. He was sighing for the golden age; let him walk to it. Every step brings him nearer. The youth of the world is but a few days' journey distant. Indeed, I know persons who think they have walked back to that fresh aforetime of a single bright Sunday in autumn or early spring. Before noon they felt its airs upon their cheeks, and by nightfall, on the banks of some quiet stream, or along some path in the wood, or on some hilltop, aver they have heard the voices and felt the wonder and the mystery that so enchanted the early races of men.

I think if I could walk through a country I should not only see many things and have adventures that I should otherwise miss, but that I should come into relations with that country at first hand, and with the men and women in it, in a way that would afford the deepest satisfaction. Hence I envy

the good fortune of all walkers, and feel like joining myself to every tramp that comes along. I am jealous of the clergyman I read about the other day who footed it from Edinburgh to London, as poor Effie Deans did, carrying her shoes in her hand most of the way, and over the ground that rugged Ben Jonson strode, larking it to Scotland, so long ago. I read with longing of the pedestrian feats of college youths, so gay and light-hearted, with their coarse shoes on their feet and their knapsacks on their backs. It would have been a good draught of the rugged cup to have walked with Wilson the ornithologist, deserted by his companions, from Niagara to Philadelphia through the snows of winter. I almost wish that I had been born to the career of a German mechanic, that I might have had that delicious adventurous year of wandering over my country before I settled down to work. I think how much richer and firmer-grained life would be to me if I could journey afoot through Florida and Texas, or follow the windings of the Platte or the Yellowstone, or stroll through Oregon, or browse for a season about Canada. In the bright inspiring days of autumn I only want the time and the companion to walk back to the natal spot, the family nest, across two States and into the mountains of a third. What adventures we would have by the way, what hard pulls, what prospects from hills, what spectacles we would behold of night and day, what passages with dogs, what glances, what peeps into windows, what characters we should fall in with, and

how seasoned and hardy we should arrive at our destination!

For companion I should want a veteran of the war! Those marches put something into him I like. Even at this distance his mettle is but little softened. As soon as he gets warmed up it all comes back to him. He catches your step and away you go, a gay, adventurous, half-predatory couple. How quickly he falls into the old ways of jest and anecdote and song! You may have known him for years without having heard him hum an air, or more than casually revert to the subject of his experience during the war. You have even questioned and cross-questioned him without firing the train you wished. But get him out on a vacation tramp, and you can walk it all out of him. By the camp-fire at night, or swinging along the streams by day, song, anecdote, adventure, come to the surface, and you wonder how your companion has kept silent so long.

It is another proof of how walking brings out the true character of a man. The devil never yet asked his victims to take a walk with him. You will not be long in finding your companion out. All disguises will fall away from him. As his pores open his character is laid bare. His deepest and most private self will come to the top. It matters little whom you ride with, so he be not a pickpocket; for both of you will, very likely, settle down closer and firmer in your reserve, shaken down like a measure of corn by the jolting as the journey proceeds. But walking is a more vital copartnership; the relation

is a closer and more sympathetic one, and you do not feel like walking ten paces with a stranger without speaking to him.

Hence the fastidiousness of the professional walker in choosing or admitting a companion, and hence the truth of a remark of Emerson that you will generally fare better to take your dog than to invite your neighbor. Your cur-dog is a true pedestrian, and your neighbor is very likely a small politician. The dog enters thoroughly into the spirit of the enterprise; he is not indifferent or preoccupied; he is constantly sniffing adventure, laps at every spring, looks upon every field and wood as a new world to be explored, is ever on some fresh trail, knows some-. thing important will happen a little farther on, gazes with the true wonder-seeing eyes, whatever the spot or whatever the road finds it good to be there, — in short, is just that happy, delicious, excursive vagabond that touches one at so many points, and whose human prototype in a companion robs miles and leagues of half their power to fatigue.

Persons who find themselves spent in a short walk to the market or the post-office, or to do a little shopping, wonder how it is that their pedestrian friends can compass so many weary miles and not fall down from sheer exhaustion; ignorant of the fact that the walker is a kind of projectile that drops far or near according to the expansive force of the motive that set it in motion, and that it is easy enough to regulate the charge according to the distance to be traversed. If I am loaded to carry

only one mile and am compelled to walk three, I generally feel more fatigue than if I had walked six under the proper impetus of preadjusted resolution. In other words, the will or corporeal mainspring, whatever it be, is capable of being wound up to different degrees of tension, so that one may walk all day nearly as easy as half that time if he is prepared beforehand. He knows his task, and he measures and distributes his powers accordingly. It is for this reason that an unknown road is aways a long road. We cannot cast the mental eye along it and see the end from the beginning. We are fighting in the dark, and cannot take the measure of our foe. Every step must be preordained and provided for in the mind. Hence also the fact that to vanquish one mile in the woods seems equal to compassing three in the open country. The furlongs are ambushed, and we magnify them.

Then, again, how annoying to be told it is only five miles to the next place when it is really eight or ten! We fall short nearly half the distance, and are compelled to urge and roll the spent ball the rest of the way. In such a case walking degenerates from a fine art to a mechanic art; we walk merely; to get over the ground becomes the one serious and engrossing thought; whereas success in walking is not to let your right foot know what your left foot doeth. Your heart must furnish such music that in keeping time to it your feet will carry you around the globe without knowing it. The walker I would describe takes no note of distance;

his walk is a sally, a honnnot^ an unspoken jeu d^esprit; the ground is his butt, his provocation; it furnishes him the resistance his body craves; he rebounds upon it, he glances off and returns again, and uses it gayly as his tool,

I do not think I exaggerate the importance or the charms of pedestrianism, or our need as a people to cultivate the art. I think it would tend to soften the national manners, to teach us the meaning of leisure, to acquaint us with the charms of the open air, to strengthen and foster the tie between the race and the land. No one else looks out upon the world so kindly and charitably as the pedestrian; no one else gives and takes so much from the country he passes through. Next to the laborer in the fields, the walker holds the closest relation to the soil; and he holds a closer and more vital relation to nature because he is freer and his mind more at leisure.

Man takes root at his feet, and at best he is no more than a potted plant in his house or carriage till he has established communication with the soil by the loving and magnetic touch of his soles to it. Then the tie of association is born; then spring those invisible fibres and rootlets through which character comes to smack of the soil, and which make a man kindred to the spot of earth he inhabits.

The roads and paths you have walked along in summer and winter weather, the fields and hills which you have looked upon in lightness and gladness of heart, where fresh thoughts have come into

your mind, or some noble prospect has opened before you, and especially the quiet ways where you have walked in sweet converse with your friend, pausing under the trees, drinking at the spring, — henceforth they are not the same; a new charm is added; those thoughts spring there perennial, your friend walks there forever.

We have produced some good walkers and saun-terers, and some noted climbers; but as a staple recreation, as a daily practice, the mass of the people dislike and despise walking. Thoreau said he was a good horse, but a poor roadster. I chant the virtues of the roadster as well. I sing of the sweetness of gravel, good sharp quartz-grit. It is the proper condiment for the sterner seasons, and many a human gizzard would be cured of half its ills by a suitable daily allowance of it. I think Thoreau himself would have profited immensely by it. His diet was too exclusively vegetable. A man cannot live on grass alone. If one has been a lotus-eater all summer, he must turn gravel-eater in the fall and winter. Those who have tried it know that gravel possesses an equal though an opposite charm. It spurs to action. The foot tastes it and henceforth rests not. The joy of moving and surmounting, of attrition and progression, the thirst for space, for miles and leagues of distance, for sights and proi^pects, to cross mountains and thread rivers, and defy frost, heat, snow, danger, difficulties, seizes it; and from that day forth its possessor ia enrolled in the noble army of walkers.

THE SNOW-WALKERS

"T TE who marvels at the beauty of the world in summer will find equal cause for wonder and admiration in winter. It is true the pomp and the pageantry are swept away, but the essential elements remain, — the day and the night, the mountain and the valley, the elemental play and succession and the perpetual presence of the infinite sky. In winter the stars seem to have rekindled their fires, the moon achieves a fuller triumph, and the heavens wear a look of a more exalted simplicity. Summer is more wooing and seductive, more versatile and human, appeals to the aff'ections and the sentiments, and fosters inquiry and the art impulse. Winter is of a more heroic cast, and addresses the intellect. The severe studies and disciplines come easier in winter. One imposes larger tasks upon himself, and is less tolerant of his own weaknesses.

The tendinous part of the mind, so to speak, is more developed in winter; the fleshy, in summer. I should say winter had given the bone and sinew to Literature, summer the tissues and blood.

The simplicity of winter has a deep moral. The return of nature, after such a career of splendor and

prodigality, to habits so simple and austere, is not lost either upon the head or the heart. It is the philosopher coming back from the banquet and the wine to a cup of water and a crust of bread.

And then this beautiful masquerade of the elements, — the novel disguises our nearest friends put on! Here is another rain and another dew, water that will not flow, nor spill, nor receive the taint of an unclean vessel. And if we see truly, the same old beneficence and willingness to serve lurk beneath all.

Look up at the miracle of the falling snow, — the air a dizzy maze of whirling, eddying flakes, noiselessly transforming the world, the exquisite crystals dropping in ditch and gutter, and disguising in the same suit of spotless livery all objects upon which they fall. How novel and fine the first drifts! The old, dilapidated fence is suddenly set off with the most fantastic ruffles, scalloped and fluted after an unheard-of fashion! Looking down a long line of decrepit stone wall, in the trimming of which the wind had fairly run riot, I saw, as for the first time, what a severe yet master artist old Winter is. Ah, a severe artist! How stern the woods look, dark and cold and as rigid against the horizon as iron!

All life and action upon the snow have an added emphasis and significance. Every expression is underscored. Summer has few finer pictures than this winter one of the farmer foddering his cattle from a stack upon the clean snow, — the movement, the

sharply-defined figures, the great green flakes of hay, the long file of patient cows, the advance just arriving and pressing eagerly for the choicest morsels, and the bounty and providence it suggests. Or the chopper in the woods, — the prostrate tree, the white new chips, scattered about, his easy triumph over the cold, coat hanging to a limb, and the clear, sharp ring of his axe. The woods are rigid and tense, keyed up by the frost, and resound like a stringed instrument. Or the road-breakers, sallying forth with oxeri and sleds in the still, white world, the day after the storm, to restore the lost track and demolish the beleaguering drifts.

All sounds are sharper in winter; the air transmits better. At night I hear more distinctly the steady roar of the North Mountain. In summer it is a sort of complacent purr, as the breezes stroke down its sides; but in winter always the same low, sullen growl.

A severe artist! No longer the canvas and the pigments, but the marble and the chisel. When the nights are calm and the moon full, I go out to gaze upon the wonderful purity of the moonlight and the snow. The air is full of latent fire, and the cold warms me — after a different fashion from that of the kitchen stove. The world lies about me in a "trance of snow." The clouds are pearly and iridescent, and seem the farthest possible remove from the condition of a storm, — the ghosts of clouds, the indwelling beauty freed from all dross. I see the hills, bulging with great drifts, lift them-

selves up cold and white against the sky, the black lines of fences here and there obliterated by the depth of the snow. Presently a fox barks away up next the mountain, and I imagine I can almost see him sitting there, in his furs, upon the illuminated surface, and looking down in my direction. As I listen, one answers him from behind the woods in the valley. What a wild winter sound, wild and weird, up among the ghostly hills! Since the wolf has ceased to howl upon these mountains, and the panther to scream, there is nothing to be compared with it. So wild! I get up in the middle of the night to hear it. It is refreshing to the ear, and one delights to know that such wild creatures are among us. At this season Nature makes the most of every throb of life that can withstand her severity. How heartily she indorses this fox! In what bold relief stand out the lives of all walkers of the snow! The snow is a great tell-tale, and blabs as effectually as it obliterates. I go into the woods, and know all that has happened. I cross the fields, and if only a mouse has visited his neighbor the fact is chronicled.

The red fox is the only species that abounds in my locality; the little gray fox seems to prefer a more rocky and precipitous country, and a less rigorous climate; the cross fox is occasionally seen, and there are traditions of the silver gray among the oldest hunters. But the red fox is the sportsman's prize, and the only fur-bearer worthy of note in these mountains.^ I go out in the morning, after 1 A spur of the Catskills.

a fresh fall of snow, and see at all points where he has crossed the road. Here he has leisurely passed within rifle-range of the house, evidently reconnoitring the premises with an eye to the hen-roost. That clear, sharp track, — there is no mistaking it for the clumsy footprint of a little dog. All his wildness and agility are photographed in it. Here he has taken fright, or suddenly recollected an engagement, and in long, graceful leaps, barely touching the fence, has gone careering up the hill as fleet as the wind.

The wild, buoyant creature, how beautiful he is! I had often seen his dead carcass, and at a distance had witnessed the hounds drive him across the upper fields; but the thrill and excitement of meeting him in his wild freedom in the woods were unknown to me till, one cold winter day, drawn thither by the baying of a hound, I stood near the summit of the mountain, waiting a renewal of the sound, that I might determine the course of the dog and choose my position, — stimulated by the ambition of all young Nimrods to bag some notable game. Long I waited, and patiently, till, chilled and benumbed, I was about to turn back, when, hearing a slight noise, I looked up and beheld a most superb fox, loping along with inimitable grace and ease, evidently disturbed, but not pursued by the hound, and so absorbed in his private meditations that he failed to see me, though I stood transfixed with amazement and admiration, not ten yards distant. I took his measure at a glance, — a large male, with

dark legs, and massive tail tipped with white, a most magnificent creature; but so astonished and fascinated was I by this sudden appearance and matchless beauty, that not till I had caught the last glimpse of him, as he disappeared over a knoll, did I awake to my duty as a sportsman, and realize what an opportunity to distinguish myself I had unconsciously let slip. I clutched my gun, half angrily, as if it was to blame, and went home out of humor with myself and all fox-kind. But I have since thought better of the experience, and concluded that I bagged the game after all, the best part of it, and fleeced Eeynard of something more valuable than his fur, without his knowledge.

This is thoroughly a winter sound, — this voice of the hound upon the mountain, — and one that is music to many ears. The long trumpet-like bay, heard for a mile or more, —now faintly back to the deep recesses of the mountain, — now distinct, but still faint, as the hound comes over some prominent point and the wind favors, —anon entirely lost in the gully, — then breaking out again much nearer, and growing more and more pronounced as the dog approaches, till, when he comes around the brow of the mountain, directly above you, the barking is loud and sharp. On,he goes along the northern spur, his voice rising and sinking as the wind and the lay of the ground modify it, till lost to hearing.

The fox usually keeps half a mile ahead, regulating his speed by tKat of the hound, occasionally pausing a moment to divert himself with a mouse.

or to contemplate the landscape, or to listen for his pursuer. If the hound press him too closely, he leads off from mountain to mountain, and so generally escapes the hunter; but if the pursuit be slow, he plays about some ridge or peak, and falls a prey, though not an easy one, to the experienced sportsman.

A most spirited and exciting chase occurs when the farm-dog gets close upon one in the open field, as sometimes happens in the early morning. The fox relies so confidently upon his superior speed, that I imagine he half tempts the dog to the race. But if the dog be a smart one, and their course lies down hill, over smooth ground, Eeynard must put his best foot forward, and then sometimes suffer the ignominy of being run over by his pursuer, who, however, is quite unable to pick him up, owing to the speed. But when they mount the hill, or enter the woods, the superior nimbleness and agility of the fox tell at once, and he easily leaves the dog far in his rear. For a cur less than his own size he manifests little fear, especially if the two meet alone, remote from the house. In such cases, I have seen first one turn tail, then the other.

A novel spectacle often occurs in summer, when the female has young. You are rambling on the mountain, accompanied by your dog, when you are startled by that wild, half-threatening squall, and in a moment perceive your dog, with inverted tail, and shame and confusion in his looks, sneaking toward you, the old fox but a few rods in his rear.

You speak to him sharply, when he bristles up, turns about, and, barking, starts off vigorously, as if to wipe out the dishonor; but in a moment comes sneaking back more abashed than ever, and owns himself unworthy to be called a dog. The fox fairly shames him out of the woods. The secret of the matter is her sex, though her conduct, for the honor of the fox be it said, seems to be prompted only by solicitude for the safety of her young.

One of the most notable features of the fox is his large and massive tail. Seen running on the snow at a distance, his tail is quite as conspicuous as his body; and, so far from appearing a burden, seems to contribute to his lightness and buoyancy. It softens the outline of his movements, and repeats or continues to the eye the ease and poise of his carriage. But, pursued by the hound on a wet, thawy day, it often becomes so heavy and bedraggled as to prove a serious inconvenience, and compels him to take refuge in his den. He is very loath to do this; both his pride and the traditions of his race stimulate him to run it out, and win by fair superiority of wind and speed; and only a wound or a heavy and moppish tail will drive him to avoid the issue in this manner.

To learn his surpassing shrewdness and cunning, attempt to take him with a trap. Rogue that he is, he always suspects some trick, and one must be more of a fox than he is himself to overreach him. M first sight it would appear easy enough. AVith apparent indifference he crosses your path, or walks

in your footsteps in the field, or travels along the beaten highway, or lingers in the vicinity of stacks and remote barns. Carry the carcass of a pig, or a fowl, or a dog, to a distant field in midwinter, and in a few nights his tracks cover the snow about it.

The inexperienced country youth, misled by this seeming carelessness of Reynard, suddenly conceives a project to enrich himself with fur, and wonders that the idea has not occurred to him before, and to others. I knew a youthful yeoman of this kind, who imagined he had found a mine of wealth on discovering on a remote side-hill, between two woods, a dead porker, upon which it appeared all the foxes of the neighborhood had nightly banqueted. The clouds were burdened with snow; and as the first flakes commenced to eddy down, he set out, trap and broom in hand, already counting over in imagination the silver quarters he would receive for his first fox-skin. With the utmost care, and with a palpitating heart, he removed enough of the trodden snow to allow the trap to sink below the surface. Then, carefully sifting the light element over it and sweeping his tracks full, he quickly withdrew, laughing exultingly over the little surprise he had prepared for the cunning rogue. The elements conspired to aid him, and the falling snow rapidly obliterated all vestiges of his work. The next morning at dawn he was on his way to bring in his fur. The snow had done its work effectually, and, he believed, had kept his secret well. Arrived in sight of the locality, he strained his vision to make out

his prize lodged against the fence at the foot of the hill. Approaching nearer, the surface was unbroken, and doubt usurped the place of certainty in his mind. A slight mound marked the site of the porker, but there was no footprint near it. Looking up the hill, he saw where Keynard had walked leisurely down toward his wonted bacon till within a few yards of it, when he had wheeled, and with prodigious strides disappeared in the woods. The young trapper saw at a glance what a comment this was upon his skill in the art, and, indignantly exhuming the iron, he walked home with it, the stream of silver quarters suddenly setting in another direction.

The successful trapper commences in the fall, or before the first deep snow. In a field not too remote, with an old axe he cuts a small place, say ten inches by fourteen, in the frozen ground, and removes the earth to the depth of three or four inches, then fills the cavity with dry ashes, in which are placed bits of roasted cheese. Reynard is very suspicious at first, and gives the place a wide berth. It looks like design, and he will see how the thing behaves before he approaches too near. But the cheese is savory and the cold severe. He ventures a little closer every night, until he can reach and pick a piece from the surface. Emboldened by success, like other mortals, he presently digs freely among the ashes, and, finding a fresh supply of the delectable morsels every night, is soon thrown off his guard and his suspicions quite fulled. After a week of baiting in this manner, and on the eve of a light fall of snow, the trapper carefully conceals his trap in the bed, first smoking it thoroughly with hemlock boughs to kill or neutralize all smell of the iron. If the weather favors and the proper precautions have been taken, he may succeed, though the chances are still greatly against him.

Reynard is usually caught very lightly, seldom more than the ends of his toes being between the jaws. He sometimes works so cautiously as to spring the trap without injury even to his toes, or may remove the cheese night after night without even springing it. I knew an old trapper who, on finding himself outwitted in this manner, tied a bit of cheese to the pan, and next morning had poor Reynard by the jaw. The trap is not fastened, but only incumbered with a clog, and is all the more sure in its hold by yielding to every effort of the animal to extricate himself.

When Reynard sees his captor approaching, he would fain drop into a mouse-hole to render himself invisible. He crouches to the ground and remains perfectly motionless until he perceives himself discovered, when he makes one desperate and final effort to escape, but ceases all struggling as you come up, and behaves in a manner that stamps him a very timid warrior, — cowering to the earth with a mingled look of shame, guilt, and abject fear. A young farmer told me of tracing one with his trap to the border of a wood, where he discovered the cunning rogue trying to hide by embracing a small tree. Most animals, when taken in a trap, show fight; but Reynard has more faith in the nimble-ness of his feet than in the terror of his teeth.

Entering the woods, the number and variety of the tracks contrast strongly with the rigid, frozen aspect of things. Warm jets of life still shoot and play amid this snowy desolation. Fox-tracks are far less numerous than in the fields; but those of hares, skunks, partridges, squirrels, and mice abound. The mice tracks are very pretty, and look like a sort of fantastic stitching on the coverlid of the snow. One is curious to know what brings these tiny creatures from their retreats; they do not seem to be in quest of food, but rather to be traveling about for pleasure or sociability, though always going post-haste, and linking stump with stump and tree with tree by fine, hurried strides. That is when they travel openly; but they have hidden passages and winding galleries under the snow, which undoubtedly are their main avenues of communication. Here and there these passages rise so near the surface as to be covered by only a frail arch of snow, and a slight ridge betrays their course to the eye. I know him well. He is known to the farmer as the "deer mouse," to the naturalist as the white-footed mouse, — a very beautiful creature, nocturnal in his habits, with large ears, and large, fine eyes, full of a wild, harmless look. He is daintily marked, with white feet and a white belly. When disturbed by day he is very easily captured, having none of the cunning or viciousness of the common Old World mouse.

It is he who, high in the hollow trunk of some tree, lays by a store of beechnuts for winter use. Every nut is carefully shelled, and the cavity that serves as storehouse lined with grass and leaves. The wood-chopper frequently squanders this precious store. I have seen half a peck taken from one tree, as clean and white as if put up by the most delicate hands, — as they were. How long it must have taken the little creature to collect this quantity, to hull them one by one, and convey them up to his fifth-story chamber! He is not confined to the woods, but is quite as common in the fields, particularly in the fall, amid the corn and potatoes. When routed by the plow, I have seen the old one take flight with half a dozen young hanging to her teats, and with such reckless speed that some of the young would lose their hold and fly off amid the weeds. Taking refuge in a stump with the rest of her family, the anxious mother would presently come back and hunt up the missing ones.

The snow-walkers are mostly night-walkers also, and the record they leave upon the snow is the main clew one has to their life and doings. The hare is nocturnal in its habits, and though a very lively creature at night, with regular courses and run-ways through the wood, is entirely quiet by day. Timid as he is, he makes little efl'ort to conceal himself, usually squatting beside a log, stump, or tree, and seeming to avoid rocks and ledges where he might

be partially housed from the cold and the snow, but where also — and this consideration undoubtedly determines his choice — he would be more apt to fall a prey to his enemies. In this, as well as in many other respects, he differs from the rabbit proper: he never burrows in the ground, or takes refuge in a den or hole, when pursued. If caught in the open fields, he is much confused and easily overtaken by the dog; but in the woods, he leaves him at a bound. In summer, when first disturbed, he beats the ground violently with his feet, by which means he would express to you his surprise or displeasure; it is a dumb way he has of scolding. After leaping a few yards, he pauses an instant, as if to determine the degree of danger, and then hurries away with a much lighter tread.

His feet are like great pads, and his track has little of the sharp, articulated expression of Key-nard's, or of animals that climb or dig. Yet it is very pretty like all the rest, and tells its own tale. There is nothing bold or vicious or vulpine in it, and his timid, harmless character is published at every leap. He abounds in dense woods, preferring localities filled with a small undergrowth of beech and birch, upon the bark of which he feeds. Nature is rather partial to him, and matches his extreme local habits and character with a suit that corresponds with his surroundings, — reddish gray in summer and white in winter.

The sharp-rayed track of the partridge adds another figure to this fantastic embroidery upon the

winter snow. Her course is a clear, strong line, sometimes quite wayward, but generally very direct, steering for the densest, most impenetrable places,

— leading you over logs and through brush, alert and expectant, till, suddenly, she bursts up a few

.yards from you, and goes humming through the trees, —— the complete triumph of endurance and vigor. Hardy native bird, may your tracks never be fewer, or your visits to the birch-tree less frequent !

The squirrel tracks — sharp, nervous, and wiry

— have their histories also. But who ever saw squirrels in winter? The naturalists say they are mostly torpid; yet evidently that little pocket-faced depredator, the chipmunk, was not carrying buckwheat for so many days to his hole for nothing: was he anticipating a state of torpidity, or providing against the demands of a very active appetite ? Red and gray squirrels are more or less active all Avinter, though very shy, and, I am inclined to think, partially nocturnal in their habits. Here a gray one has just passed, — came down that tree and went up this; there he dug for a beechnut, and left the burr on the snow. How did he know where to dig ? During an unusually severe winter I have known him to make long journeys to a barn, in a remote field, where wheat was stored. How did he know there was wheat there? In attempting to return, the adventurous creature was frequently run down and caught in the deep snow.

His home is in the trunk of some old birch or maple, with an entrance far up amid the branches. In the spring he builds himself a summer-house of small leafy twigs in the top of a neighboring beech, where the young are reared and much of the time passed. But the safer retreat in the maple is not abandoned, and both old and young resort thither in the fall, or when danger threatens. AVhether this temporary residence amid the branches is for elegance or pleasure, or for sanitary reasons or domestic convenience, the naturalist has forgotten to mention.

The elegant creature, so cleanly in its habits, so graceful in its carriage, so nimble and daring in its movements, excites feelings of admiration akin to those awakened by the birds and the fairer forms of nature. IIis passage through the trees is almost a flight. Indeed, the flying squirrel has little or no advantage over him, and in speed and nimbleness cannot compare with him at all. If he miss his footing and fall, he is sure to catch on the next branch; if the connection be broken, he leaps recklessly for the nearest spray or limb, and secures his hold, even if it be by the aid of his teeth.

His career of frolic and festivity begins in the fall, after the birds have left us and the holiday spirit of nature has commenced to subside. How absorbing the pastime of the sportsman who goes to the woods in the still October morning in quest of him! You step lightly across the threshold of the forest, and sit down upon the first log or rock to await the signals. It is so still that the ear sud-

denly seems to have acquired new powers, and there is no movement to confuse the eye. Presently you hear the rustling of a branch, and see it sway or spring as the squirrel leaps from or to it; or else you hear a disturbance in the dry leaves, and mark one running upon the ground. He has probably seen the intruder, and, not liking his stealthy movements, desires to avoid a nearer acquaintance. Now he mounts a stump to see if the way is clear, then pauses a moment at the foot of a tree to take his bearings, his tail, as he skims along, undulating behind him, and adding to the easy grace and dignity of his movements. Or else you are first advised of his proximity by the dropping of a false nut, or the fragments of the shucks rattling upon the leaves. Or, again, after contemplating you a while unobserved, and making up his mind that you are not dangerous, he strikes an attitude on a branch, and commences to quack and bark, with an accompanying movement of his tail. Late in the afternoon, when the same stillness reigns, the same scenes are repeated. There is a black variety, quite rare, but mating freely with the gray, from which he seems to be distinguished only in color.

The track of the red squirrel may be known by its smaller size. He is more common and less dignified than the gray, and oftener guilty of petty larceny about the barns and grain-fields. He is most abundant in old barkpeelings, and low, dilapidated hemlocks, from which he makes excursions to the fields and orchards, spinning along the tops of the fences, whicli afford not only convenient lines of communication, but a safe retreat if danger threatens. He loves to linger about the orchard; and, sitting upright on the topmost stone in the wall, or on the tallest stake in the fence, chipping up an apple for the seeds, his tail conforming to the curve of his back, his paws shifting and turning the apple, he is a pretty sight, and his bright, pert appearance atones for all the mischief he does. At home, in the woods, he is the most frolicsome and loquacious. The appearance of anything unusual, if, after contemplating it a moment, he concludes it not dangerous, excites his unbounded mirth and ridicule, and he snickers and chatters, hardly able to contain himself; now darting up the trunk of a tree and squealing in derision, then hopping into position on a limb and dancing to the music of his own cackle, and all for your special benefit.

There is something very human in this apparent mirth and mockery of the squirrels. It seems to be a sort of ironical laughter, and implies self-conscious pride and exultation in the laugher. "What a ridiculous thing you are, to be sure! *' he seems to say; "how clumsy and awkward, and what a poor show for a tail! Look at me, look at me! " — and he capers about in his best style. Again, he would seem to tease you and provoke your attention; then suddenly assumes a tone of good-natured, childlike defiance and derision. That pretty little imp, the chipmunk, will sit on the stone above his den and defy you, as plainly as if he said so, to catch him

before he can get into his hole if you can. You hurl a stone at him, and "No you didn't!" comes up from the depth of his retreat.

In February another track appears upon the snow, slender and delicate, about a third larger than that of the gray squirrel, indicating no haste or speed, but, on the contrary, denoting the most imperturbable ease and leisure, the footprints so close together that the trail appears like a chain of curiously carved links. Sir Mephitis mephitica, or, in plain English, the skunk, has woke up from his six weeks' nap, and come out into society again. He is a nocturnal traveler, very bold and impudent, coming quite up to the barn and outbuildings, and sometimes taking up his quarters for the season under the haymow. There is no such word as hurry in his dictionary, as you may see by his path upon the snow. He has a very sneaking, insinuating way, and goes creeping about the fields and woods, never once in a perceptible degree altering his gait, and, if a fence crosses his course, steers for a break or opening to avoid climbing. He is too indolent even to dig his own hole, but appropriates that of a woodchuck, or hunts out a crevice in the rocks, from which he extends his rambling in all directions, preferring damp, thawy weather. He has very little discretion or cunning, and holds a trap in utter contempt, stepping into it as soon as beside it, relying implicitly for defense against all forms of danger upon the unsavory punishment he is capable of inflicting. He is quite indifferent to both man

and beast, and will not hurry himself to get out of the way of either. Walking through the summer fields at twilight, I have come near stepping upon him, and was much the more disturbed of the two. When attacked in the open fields he confounds the plans of his enemies by the unheard-of tactics of exposing his rear rather than his front. "Come if you dare," he says, and his attitude makes even the farm-dog pause. After a few encounters of this kind, and if you entertain the usual hostility towards him, your mode of attack will speedily resolve itself into moving about him in a circle, the radius of which will be the exact distance at which you can hurl a stone with accuracy and effect.

He has a secret to keep and knows it, and is careful not to betray himself until he can do so with the most telling effect. I have known him to preserve his serenity even when caught in a steel trap, and look the very picture of injured innocence, manoeuvring carefully and deliberately to extricate his foot from the grasp of the naughty jaws. Do not by any means take pity on him, and lend a helping hand!

How pretty his face and head! How fine and delicate his teeth, like a weasel's or cat's!

When about a third grown, he looks so well that one covets him for a pet. He is quite precocious, however, and capable, even at this tender age, of making a very strong appeal to your sense of smell.

No animal is more cleanly in its habits than he. He is not an awkward boy who cuts his own face

with his whip; and neither his flesh nor his fur hints the weapon with which he is armed. The most silent creature known to me, he makes no sound, so far as I have observed, save a diffuse, impatient noise, like that produced by beating your hand with a whisk-broom, when the farm-dog has discovered his retreat in the stone .fence. He renders himself obnoxious to the farmer by his partiality for hens' eggs and young poultry. He is a confirmed epicure, and at plundering hen-roosts an expert. Not the full-grown fowls are his victims, but the youngest and most tender. At night Mother Hen receives under her maternal wings a dozen newly hatched chickens, and with much pride and satisfaction feels them all safely tucked away in her feathers. In the morning she is walking about disconsolately, attended by only two or three of all that pretty brood. What has happened? Where are they gone? That pickpocket, Sir Mephitis, could solve the mystery. Quietly has he approached, under cover of darkness, and one by one relieved her of her precious charge. Look closely and you will see their little yellow legs and beaks, or part of a mangled form, lying about on the ground. Or, before the hen has hatched, he may find her out, and, by the same sleight of hand, remove every egg, leaving only the empty blood-stained shells to witness against him. The birds, especially the ground-builders, suffer in like manner from his plundering propensities.

The secretion upon which he relies for defense,

and which is the chief source of his unpopularity, while it affords good reasons against cultivating him as a pet, and mars his attractiveness as game, is by no means the greatest indignity that can be offered to a nose. It is a rank, living smell, and has none of the sickening qualities of disease or putrefaction. Indeed, I think a good smeller will enjoy its most refined intensity. It approaches the sublime, and makes the nose tingle. It is tonic and bracing, and, I can readily believe, has rare medicinal qualities. I do not recommend its use as eyewater, though an old farmer assures me it has undoubted virtues when thus applied. Hearing, one night, a disturbance among his hens, he rushed suddenly out to catch the thief, when Sir Mephitis, taken by surprise, and no doubt much annoyed at being interrupted, discharged the vials of his wrath full in the farmer's face, and with such admirable effect that, for a few moments, he was completely blinded, and powerless to revenge himself upon the rogue, who embraced the opportunity to make good his escape; but he declared that afterwards his eyes felt as if purged by fire, and his sight was much clearer.

In March that brief summary of a bear, the raccoon, comes out of his den in the ledges, and leaves his sharp digitigrade track upon the snow, —traveling not unfrequently in pairs, — a lean, hungry couple, bent on pillage and plunder. They have an unenviable time of it, — feasting in the summer and fall, hibernating in winter, and starving in spring. In April I have found the young of the

previous year creeping about the fields, so reduced by starvation as to be quite helpless, and offering no resistance to my taking them up by the tail and carrying them home.

The old ones also become very much emaciated, and come boldly up to the barn or other outbuildings in quest of food. I remember, one morning in early spring, of hearing old Cuff, the farm-dog, barking vociferously before it was yet light. When we got up we discovered him, at the foot of an ash-tree standing about thirty rods from the house, looking up at some gray object in the leafless branches, and by his manners and his voice evincing great impatience that we were so tardy in coming to his assistance. Arrived on the spot, we saw in the tree a coon of unusual size. One bold climber proposed to go up and shake him down. This was what old Cuff wanted, and he fairly bounded with delight as he saw his young master shinning up the tree. Approaching within eight or ten feet of the coon, he seized the branch to which it clung and shook long and fiercely. But the coon was in no danger of losing its hold, and, when the climber paused to renew his hold, it turned toward him with a growl, and showed very clearly a purpose to advance to the attack. This caused his pursuer to descend to the ground again with all speed. When the coon was finally brought down with a gun, he fought the dog, which was a large, powerful animal, with great fury, returning bite for bite for some moments; and after a quarter of an hour had elapsed and his unequal

antagonist had shaken him as a terrier does a rat, making his teeth meet through the small of his back, the coon still showed fight.

They are very tenacious of life, and like the badger will always \yhip a dog of their own size and weight. A woodchuck can bite severely, having teeth that cut like chisels, but a coon has agility and power of limb as well.

They are only considered game in the fall, or towards the close of summer, when they become fat and their flesh sweet. At this time, cooning in the remote interior is a famous pastime. As this animal is entirely nocturnal in its habits, it is hunted only at night. A piece of corn on some remote side-hill near the mountain, or between two pieces of woods, is most apt to be frequented by them. While the corn is yet green they pull the ears down like hogs, and, tearing open the sheathing of husks, eat the tender, succulent kernels, bruising and destroying much more than they devour. Sometimes their ravages are a matter of serious concern to the farmer. But every such neighborhood has its coon-dog, and the boys and young men dearly love the sport. The party sets out about eight or nine o'clock of a dark, moonless night, and stealthily approach the cornfield. The dog knows his business, and when he is put into a patch of corn and told to " hunt them up" he makes a thorough search, and will not be misled by any other scent. You hear him rattling through the corn, hither and yon, with great speed. The coons prick up their ears, and leave on the

opposite side of the field. In the stillness you may sometimes hear a single stone rattle on the wall as they hurry toward the woods. If the dog finds nothing he comes back to his master in a short time, and says in his dumb way, "No coon there." But if he strikes a trail you presently hear a louder rattling on the stone wall, and then a hurried bark as he enters the woods, followed in a few minutes by loud and repeated barking as he reaches the foot of the tree in which the coon has taken refuge. Then follows a pellmell rush of the cooning party up the hill, into the woods, through the brush and the darkness, falling over prostrate trees, pitching into gullies and hollows, losing hats and tearing clothes, till finally, guided by the baying of the faithful dog, the tree is reached. The first thing now in order is to kindle a fire, and, if its light reveals the coon, to shoot him; if not, to fell the tree with an axe. If this happens to be too great a sacrifice of timber and of strength, to sit down at the foot of the tree till morning.

But with March our interest in these phases of animal life, which winter has so emphasized and brought out, begins to decline. Vague rumors are afloat in the air of a great and coming change. We are eager for Winter to be gone, since he, too, is fugitive and cannot keep his place. Invisible hands deface his icy statuary; his chisel has lost its cunning. The drifts, so pure and exquisite, are now earth-stained and weather-worn, —the flutes and scallops, and fine, firm lines, all gone; and what was a grace and an ornament to the hills is now a disfiguration. Like worn and unwashed linen appear the remains of that spotless robe with which he clothed the world as his bride.

But he will not abdicate without a struggle. Day-after day he rallies his scattered forces, and night after night pitches his white tents on the hills, and would fain regain his lost ground; but the young prince in every encounter prevails. Slowly and reluctantly the gray old hero retreats up the mountain, till finally the south rain comes in earnest, and in a night he is dead.

THE FOX

T HAVE already spoken of the fox at some -^ length, but it will take a chapter by itself to do half justice to his portrait.

He furnishes, perhaps, the only instance that can be cited of a fur-bearing animal that not only holds its own, but that actually increases in the face of the means that are used for its extermination. The beaver, for instance, was gone before the earliest settlers could get a sight of him; and even the mink and marten are now only rarely seen, or not seen at all, in places where they were once abundant.

But the fox has survived civilization, and in some localities is no doubt more abundant now than in the time of the Revolution. For half a century at least he has been almost the only prize, in the way of fur, that was to be found on our mountains, and he has been hunted and trapped and waylaid, sought for as game and pursued in enmity, taken by fair means and by foul, and yet there seems not the slightest danger of the species becoming extinct.

One would think that a single hound in a neighborhood, filling the mountains with his hayings, and leaving no nook or byway of them unexplored, was

enough to drive and scare every fox from the country. But not so. Indeed, I am almost tempted to say, the more hounds, the more foxes.

I recently spent a summer month in a mountainous district in.the State of New York, where, from its earliest settlement, tne red fox has been the standing prize for skill in the use of the trap and gun. At the house where I was stopping were two foxhounds, and a neighbor half a mile distant had a third. There were many others in the township, and in season they were well employed, too; but the three spoken of, attended by their owners, held high carnival on the mountains in the immediate vicinity. And many were the foxes that, winter after winter, fell before them, twenty-five having been shot, the season before my visit, on one small range alone. And yet the foxes were apparently never more abundant than they were that summer, and never bolder, coming at night within a few rods of the house, and of the unchained alert hounds, and making havoc among the poultry.

One morning a large, fat goose was found minus her head and otherwise mangled. Both hounds had disappeared, and, as they did not come back till near night, it was inferred that they had cut short Reynard's repast, and given him a good chase into the bargain. But next night he was back again, and this time got safely off with the goose. A couple of nights after he must have come with recruits, for next morning three large goslings were reported missing. The silly geese now got it through theii

noddles that there was danger about, and every night thereafter came close up to the house to roost.

A brood of turkeys, the old one tied to a tree a few rods to the rear of the house, were the next objects of attack. The predaceous rascal came, as usual, in the latter half of the night. I happened to be awake, and heard the helpless turkey cry "Quit," "quit," with great emphasis. Another sleeper, on the floor above me, who, it seems, had been sleeping with one ear awake for several nights in apprehension for the safety of his turkeys, heard the sound also, and instantly divined its cause. I heard the window open and a voice summon the dogs. A loud bellow was the response, which caused Keyiiard to take himself off in a hurry. A moment more, and the mother turkey would have shared the fate of the geese. There she lay at the end of her tether, with extended wings, bitten and rumpled. The young ones roosted in a row on the fence near by, and had taken flight on the first alarm.

Turkeys, retaining many of their wild instincts, are less easily captured by the fox than any other of our domestic fowls. On the slightest show of danger they take to wing, and it is not unusual, in the locality of which I speak, to find them in the morning perched in the most unwonted places, as on the peak of the barn or hay-shed, or on the tops of the apple-trees, their tails spread and their manners showing much excitement. Perchance one turkey is minus her tail, the fox having succeeded in getting only a mouthful of quills.

As the brood grows and their wings develop, they wander far from the house in quest of grasshoppers. At such times they are all watchfulness and suspicion. Crossing the fields one day, attended by a dog that much resembled a fox, I came suddenly upon a brood about one third grown, which were feeding in a pasture just beyond a wood. It so happened that they caught sight of the dog without seeing me, when instantly, with the celerity of wild game, they launched into the air, and, while the old one perched upon a treetop, as if to keep an eye on the supposed enemy, the young went sailing over the trees toward home.

The two hounds above referred to, accompanied by a cur-dog, whose business it was to mind the farm, but who took as much delight in running away from prosy duty as if he had been a schoolboy, would frequently steal off and have a good hunt all by themselves, just for the fun of the thing, I suppose. I more than half suspect that it was as a kind of taunt or retaliation, that Keynard came and took the geese from under their very noses. One morning they went off and stayed till the afternoon of the next day; they ran the fox all day and all night, the hounds baying at every jump, the cur-dog silent and tenacious. When the trio returned they came dragging themselves along, stiff, footsore, gaunt, and hungry. For a day or two afterward they lay about the kennels, seeming to dread nothing so much as the having to move. The stolen hunt was their "spree," their "bender," and of course they must take time to get over it.

Some old hunters think the fox enjoys the chase as much as the hound, especially when the latter runs slow, as the best hounds do. The fox will wait for the hound, will sit down and listen, or play about, crossing and recrossing and doubling upon his track, as if enjoying a mischievous consciousness of the perplexity he would presently cause his pursuer. It is evident, however, that the fox does not always have his share of the fun: before a swift dog, or in a deep snow, or on a wet day when his tail gets heavy, he must put his best foot forward. As a last resort he "holes up." Sometimes he resorts to numerous devices to mislead and escape the dog altogether. He will walk in the bed of a small creek, or on a rail-fence. I heard of an instance of a fox, hard and long pressed, that took to a rail-fence, and, after walking some distance, made a leap to one side to a hollow stump, in the cavity of which he snugly stowed himself. The ruse succeeded, and the dogs lost the trail; but the hunter, coming up, passed by chance near the stump, when out bounded the fox, his cunning availing him less than he deserved. On another occasion the fox took to the public road, and stepped with great care and precision into a sleigh-track. The hard, polished snow took no imprint of the light foot, and the scent was no doubt less than it would have been on a rougher surface. Maybe, also, the rogue. had considered the chances of another sleigh coming along, before the hound, and obliterating the trail entirely.

Audubon relates of a certain fox, which, when started by the hounds, always managed to elude them at a certain point. Finally the hunter concealed himself in the locality, to discover, if possible, the trick. Presently along came the fox, and, making a leap to one side, ran up the trunk of a fallen tree which had lodged some feet from the ground, and concealed himself in the top. In a few minutes the hounds came up, and in their eagerness passed some distance beyond the point, and then went still farther, looking for the lost trail. Then the fox hastened down, and, taking his backtrack, fooled the dogs completely.

I was told of a silver-gray fox in northern New York, which, when pursued by the hounds, would run till it had hunted up another fox, or the fresh trail of one, when it would so manoeuvre that the hound would invariably be switched ofif on the second track.

In cold, dry weather the fox will sometimes elude the hound, at least delay him much, by taking to a bare, plowed field. The hard dry earth seems not to retain a particle of the scent, and the hound gives a loud, long, peculiar bark, to signify he has trouble. It is now his turn to show his wit, which he often does by passing completely around the field, and resuming the trail again where it crosses the fence or a strip of snow.

The fact that any dry, hard surfacc is unfavorable to the hound, suggests, in a measure, the explanation of the wonderful faculty that all dogs in a degree possess to track an animal by the scent of the foot alone. Did you ever think why a dog's nose is always wet ? Examine the nose of a foxhound, for instance; how very moist and sensitive! Cause this moisture to dry up, and the dog would be as powerless to track an animal as you are! The nose of the cat, you may observe, is but a little moist, and, as you know, her sense of smell is far inferior to that of the dog. Moisten your own nostrils and lips, and this sense is plainly sharpened. The sweat of a dog's nose, therefore, is no doubt a vital element in its power, and, without taking a very long logical stride, we may infer how a damp, rough surface aids him in tracking game.

A fox hunt in this country is, of course, quite a different thing from what it is in England, where all the squires and noblemen of a borough, superbly mounted, go riding over the country, guided by the yelling hounds, till the fox is literally run down and murdered. Here the hunter prefers a rough, mountainous country, and, as probably most persons know, takes advantage of the disposition of the fox, when pursued by the hound, to play or circle around a ridge or bold point, and, taking his stand near the run-way shoots him down.

I recently had the pleasure of a turn with some experienced hunters. As we ascended the ridge toward the mountain, keeping in our ears the uncer-

tain baying of the hounds as they slowly unraveled an old trail, my companions pointed out to me the different run-ways, — a gap in the fence here, a rock just below the brow of the hill there, that tree yonder near the corner of the woods, or the end of that stone wall looking down the side-hill, or commanding a cow path, or the outlet of a wood-road. A half wild apple orchard near a cross road was pointed out as an invariable run-way, where the fox turn#d toward the mountain again, after having been driven down the ridge. There appeared to be no reason why the foxes should habitually pass any particular point, yet the hunters told me that year after year they took about the same turns, each generation of foxes running through the upper corner of that field, or crossing the valley near yonder stone wall, when pursued by the dog. It seems the fox when he finds himself followed is perpetually tempted to turn in his course, to deflect from a right line, as a person would undoubtedly be under similar circumstances. If he is on this side of the ridge, when he hears the dog break around on his trail he speedily crosses to the other side; if he is in the fields he takes again to the woods; if in the valley he hastens to the high land, and evidently enjoys running along the ridge and listening to the dogs, slowly tracing out his course in the fields below. At such times he appears to have but one sense, hearing, and that reverted toward his pursuers. He is constantly pausing, looking back and listening, and will almost run over the hunter if he stands still, even though not at all concealed.

Animals of this class depend far less upon their sight than upon their hearing and sense of smell. Neither the fox nor the dog is capable of much discrimination with the eye; they seem to see things only in the mass; but with the nose they can analyze and define, and get at the most subtle shades of difference. The fox will not read a man from a stump or a rock, unless he gets his scent, and the dog does not know his master in a crowd until he has smelled him.

On the occasion to which I refer, it was not many minutes after the dogs entered the woods on the side of the mountain before they gave out sharp and eager, and we knew at once that the fox was started. We were then near a point that had been designated as a sure run-way, and hastened to get into position with all speed. For my part I was so taken with the music of the hounds, as it swelled up over the ridge, that I quite forgot the game. I saw one of my companions leveling his gun, and, looking a few rods to the right, saw the fox coming right on to us. I had barely time to note the silly and abashed expression that came over him as he saw us in his path, when he was cut down as by a flash of lightning. The rogue did not appear frightened, but ashamed and out of countenance, as one does when some trick has been played upon him, or when detected in some mischief.

Late in the afternoon, as we were passing through a piece of woods in the valley below, another fox, the third that day, broke from his cover in an old

treetop, under our very noses, and drew the fire of three of our party, myself among the number, but, thanks to the interposing trees and limbs, escaped unhurt. Then the dogs took up the trail and there was lively music again. The fox steered through the fields direct for the ridge where we had passed up in the morning. We knew he would take a turn here and then point for the mountain, and two of us, with the hope of cutting him off by the old orchard, through which we were again assured he would surely pass, made a precipitous rush for that point. It was nearly half a mile distant, most of the way up a steep side-hill, and if the fox took the circuit indicated he would probably be there in twelve or fifteen minutes. Running up an angle of 45° seems quite easy v»rork for a four-footed beast like a dog or fox, but to a two-legged animal like a man it is very heavy and awkward. Before I got half way up there seemed to be a vacuum all about me, so labored was my breathing, and when I reached the summit my head swam and my knees were about giving out; but pressing on, I had barely time to reach a point in the road abreast of the orchard, when I heard the hounds, and, looking under the trees, saw the fox, leaping high above the weeds and grass, coming straight toward me. He evidently had not got over the first scare, which our haphazard fusillade had given him, and was making unusually quick time. I was armed with a rifle, and said to myself now was the time to win the laurels I had coveted. For half a day previous I

had been practicing on a pumpkin which a patient youth had rolled down a hill for me, and had improved my shot considerably. Now a yellow pumpkin was coming which was not a pumpkin, and for the first time during the day opportunity favored me. I expected the fox to cross the road a few yards below me, but just then I heard him whisk through the grass, and he bounded upon the fence a few yards above. He seemed to cringe as he saw his old enemy, and to depress his fur to half his former dimensions. Three bounds and he had cleared the road, when my bullet tore up the sod beside him, but to this hour I do not know whether I looked at the fox without seeing my gun, or whether I did sight him across its barrel. I only know that I did not distinguish myself in the use of the rifle on that occasion, and went home to wreak my revenge upon another pumpkin; but without much improvement of my skill, for, a few days after, another fox ran under my very nose with perfect impunity. There is something so fascinating in the sudden appearance of the fox that the eye is quite mastered, and, unless the instinct of the sportsman is very strong and quick, the prey will slip through his grasp.

A still hunt rarely brings you in sight of a fox, as his ears are much sharper than yours, and his tread much lighter. But if the fox js mousing in the fields, and you discover him before he does you, you may, the wind favoring, call him within a few paces of you. Secrete yourself behind the

fence, or some other object, and squeak as nearly like a mouse as possible. E-eynard will hear the sound at an incredible distance. Pricking up his ears, he gets the direction, and comes trotting along as unsuspiciously as can be. I have never had an opportunity to try the experiment, but I know perfectly reliable persons who have. One man, in the pasture getting his cows, called a fox which was too busy mousing to get the first sight, till it jumped upon the wall just over where he sat secreted. Giving a loud whoop and jumping up at the same time, the fox came as near being frightened out of his skin as I suspect a fox ever was.

In trapping for the fox, you get perhaps about as much "fun" and as little fur as in any trapping amusement you can engage in. The one feeling that ever seems present to the mind of Keynard is suspicion. He does not need experience to teach him, but seems to know from the jump that there is such a thing as a trap, and that a trap has a way of grasping a fox's paw that is more frank than friendly. Cornered in a hole or den, a trap can be set so that the poor creature has the desperate alternative of being caught or starve. He is generally caught, though not till he has braved hunger for a good many days.

But to know all his cunning and shrewdness, bait him in the field, or set your trap by some carcass where he is wont to come. In some cases he will uncover the trap, and leave the marks of his con-

tempt for it in a way you cannot mistake, or else he will not approach within a rod of it. Occasionally, however, he finds in a trapper more than his match, and is fairly caught. When this happens, the trap, which must be of the finest make, is never touched with the bare hand, but, after being thoroughly smoked and greased, is set in a bed of dry ashes or chaff in a remote field, where the fox has been emboldened to dig for several successive nights for morsels of toasted cheese.

A light fall of snow aids the trapper's art and conspires to Reynard's ruin. But how lightly he is caught, when caught at all! barely the end of his toes, or at most a spike through the middle of his foot. I once saw a large painting of a fox struggling with a trap which held him by the hind leg, above the gambrel-joint! A painting alongside of it represented a peasant driving an ox-team from the off-side! A fox would be as likely to be caught above the gambrel-joint as a farmer would to drive his team from the off-side. I knew one that was caught by the tip of the lower jaw. He came nightly, and took the morsel of cheese from the pan of the trap without springing it. A piece was then secured to the pan by a thread, with the result as above stated.

I have never been able to see clearly why the mother fox generally selects a burrow or hole in the open field in which to have her young, except it be, as some hunters maintain, for better security. The young foxes are wont to come out on a warm day,

and- play like puppies in front of the den. The view being unobstructed on all sides by trees or bushes, in the cover of w^hich danger might approach, they are less liable to surprise and capture. On the slightest sound they disappear in the hole. Those who have watched the gambols of the young foxes speak of them as very amusing, even more arch and playful than those of kittens, while a spirit profoundly wise and cunning seems to look out of their young eyes. The parent fox can never be caught in the den with them, but is hovering near the woods, which are always at hand, and by her warning cry or bark telling them when to be on their guard. She usually has at least three dens, at no great distance apart, and moves stealthily in the night with her charge from one to the other, so as to mislead her enemies. Many a party of boys, and of men, too, discovering the whereabouts of a litter, have gone with shovels and picks, and, after digging away vigorously for several hours, have found only an empty hole for their pains. The old fox, finding her secret had been found out, had waited for darkness, in the cover of which to transfer her household to new quarters; or else some old fox-hunter, jealous of the preservation of his game, and getting word of the intended destruction of the litter, had gone at dusk the night before, and made some disturbance about the den, perhaps flashed some powder in its mouth, — a hint which the shrewd animal knew how to interpret.

The more scientific aspects of the question may

not be without interest to some of niy readers. The fox belongs to the great order of flesh-eating animals called Carnivoi^a, and of the family called Canidw, or dogs. The wolf is a kind of wild dog, and the fox is a kind of wolf. Foxes, unlike wolves, however, never go in packs or companies, but hunt singly. The fox has a kind of bark, which suggests the dog, as have all the members of this family. The kinship is further shown by the fact that during certain periods, for the most part in the summer, the dog cannot be made to attack or even pursue the female fox, but will run from her in the most shamefaced manner, which he will not do in the case of any other animal except a wolf. Many of the ways and manners of the fox, when tamed, are also like the dog's. I once saw a young red fox exposed for sale in the market in Washington. A colored man had him, and said he had caught him out in Virginia. He led him by a small chain, as he would a puppy, and the innocent young rascal would lie on his side and bask and sleep in the sunshine, amid all the noise and chaffering around him, precisely like a dog. He was about the size of a full-grown cat, and there was a bewitching beauty about him that I could hardly resist. On another occasion, I saw a gray fox, about two thirds grown, playing with a dog, about the same size, and by nothing in the manners of either could you tell which was the dog and which was the fox.

Some naturalists think there are but two permanent species of the fox in the United States, namely,

the gray fox and the red fox, though there are five or six varieties. The gray fox, which is much smaller and less valuable than the red, is the Southern species, and is said to be rarely found north of Maryland, though in certain rocky localities along the Hudson they are common.

In the Southern States this fox is often hunted in the English fashion, namely, on horseback, the riders tearing through the country in pursuit till the animal is run down and caught. This is the only fox that will tree. When too closely pressed, instead of taking to a den or hole, it climbs beyond the reach of the dogs in some small tree.

The red fox is the Northern species, and is rarely found farther south than the mountainous districts of Virginia. In the Arctic regions he gives place to the Arctic fox, which most of the season is white.

The prairie fox, the cross fox, and the black or silver-gray fox, seem only varieties of the red fox, as the black squirrel breeds from the gray, and the black woodchuck is found with the brown. There is little to distinguish them from the red, except the color, though the prairie fox is said to be the larger of the two.

The cross fox is dark brown on its muzzle and extremities, with a cross of red and black on its shoulders and breast, which peculiarity of coloring, and not any trait in its character, gives it its name. They are very rare, and few hunters have ever seen one. The American Fur Company used to obtain annually from fifty to one hundred skins. The

skins formerly sold for twenty-five dollars, though I believe they now bring only about five dollars.

The black or silver-gray fox is the rarest of all, and its skin the most valuable. The Indians used to estimate it equal to forty beaver skins. The great fur companies seldom collect in a single season more than four or five skins at any one post. Most of those of the American Fur Company come from the 'head-waters of the Mississippi. One of the younger Audubons shot one in northern New York. The fox had been seen and fired at many times by the hunters of the neighborhood, and had come to have the reputation of leading a charmed life, and of being invulnerable to anything but a silver bullet. But Audubon brought her down (for it was a female) on the second trial. She had a litter of young in the vicinity, which he also dug out, and found the nest to hold three black and four red ones, which fact settled the question with him that black and. red often have the same parentage, and are in truth the same species.

The color of this fox, in a point-blank view, is black, but viewed at an angle it is a dark silver-gray, whence has arisen the notion that the black and the silver-gray are distinct varieties. The tip of the tail is always white.

In almost every neighborhood there are traditions of this fox, and it is the dream of young sportsmen; but I have yet to meet the person who has seen one. I should go well to the north, into the British Possessions, if I were bent on obtaining a specimen.

One more item from the books. From the fact that in the bone caves in this country skulls of the gray fox are found, but none of the red, it is inferred by some naturalists that the red fox is a descendant from the European species, which it resembles in form but surpasses in beauty, and its appearance on this continent comparatively of recent date.

A MARCH CHRONICLE

ON THE POTOMAC

ny^ARCH 1. — The first day of spring and the -^^-^ first spring day! I felt the change the moment I put my head out of doors in the morning. A fitful, gusty south wind was blowing, though the sky was clear. But the sunlight was not the same. There was an interfusion of a new element. Kot ten days before there had been a day just as bright, — even brighter and warmer, — a clear, crystalline day of February, with nothing vernal in it; but this day was opaline; there was a film, a sentiment in it, a nearer approach to life. Then there was that fresh, indescribable odor, a breath from the Gulf, or from Florida and the Carolinas, — a subtle, persuasive influence that thrilled the sense. Every root and rootlet under ground must have felt it; the buds of the soft maple and silver poplar felt it, and swelled perceptibly during the day. The robins knew it, and were here that morning; so were the crow blackbirds. The shad must have known it, down deep in their piarine retreats, and leaped and sported about the mouths of the rivers,

ready to dart up them if the genial influence continued. The bees in the hive also, or in the old tree in the woods, no doubt awoke to new life; and the hibernating animals, the bears and woodchucks, rolled up in their subterranean dens, — I imagine the warmth reached even "^hem, and quickened their sluggish circulation.

Then in the afternoon there was the smell of smoke, — the first spring fires in the open air. The Virginia farmer is raking together the rubbish in his garden, or in the field he is preparing for the plow, and burning it up. In imagination I am there to help him. I see the children playing about, delighted with the sport and the resumption of work; the smoke goes up through the shining haze; the farmhouse door stands open, and lets in the afternoon sun; the cow lows for her calf, or hides it in the woods; and in the morning the geese, sporting in the spring sun, answer the call of the wild flock steering northward above them.

As I stroll through the market I see the signs here. That old colored woman has brought spring in her basket in those great green flakes of moss, with arbutus showing the pink; and her old man is just in good time with his fruit-trees and gooseberry bushes. Various bulbs and roots are also being brought out and off'ered, and the onions are sprouting on the stands. I see bunches of robins and cedar-birds also, — so much melody and beauty cut off from the supply going north. The fish market is beginning to be bright with perch and bass,

and with shad from the Southern rivers, and wild ducks are taking the place of prairie hens and quails.

In the Carolinas, no doubt, the fruit-trees are in bloom, and the rice land is being prepared for the seed. In the mountains of Virginia and in Ohio they are making maple sugar; in Kentucky and Tennessee they are sowing oats; in Illinois they are, perchance, husking the corn which has remained on the stalk in the field all winter. Wild geese and ducks are streaming across the sky from the lower Mississippi toward the great lakes, pausing a while on the prairies, or alighting in the great cornfields, making the air resound with the noise of their wings upon the stalks and dry shucks as they resume their journey. About this time, or a little later, in the still spring morning, the prairie hens or prairie cocks set up that low, musical cooing or crowing that defies the ear to trace or locate. The air is filled with that soft, mysterious undertone; and, save that a bird is seen here and there flitting low over the ground, the sportsman walks for hours without coming any nearer the source of the elusive sound.

All over a certain belt of the country the rivers and streams are roily, and chafe their banks. There is a movement of the soils. The capacity of the water to take up and hold in solution the salt and earths seemed never so great before. The frost has relinquished its hold, and turned everything over to the water. Mud is the mother now; and out of it creep the frogs, the turtles, the crawfish.

In the North how goes the season? The winter is perchance just breaking up. The old frost king is just striking, or preparing to strike, his tents. The ice is going out of the rivers, and the first steamboat on the Hudson is picking its way through the blue lanes and channels. The white gulls are making excursions up from the bay, to see what the prospects are. In the lumber countries, along the upper Kennebec and Penobscot, and along the northern Hudson, starters are at work with their pikes and hooks starting out the pine logs on the first spring freshet. All winter, through the deep snows, they have been hauling them to the bank of the stream, or placing them where the tide would reach them. Now, in countless numbers, beaten and bruised, the trunks of the noble trees come, borne by the angry flood. The snow that furnishes the smooth bed over which they were drawn, now melted, furnishes the power that carries them down to the mills. On the Delaware the raftsmen are at work running out their rafts. Floating islands of logs and lumber go down the swollen stream, bending over the dams, shooting through the rapids, and bringing up at last in Philadelphia or beyond.

In the inland farming districts what are the signs 1 Few and faint, but very suggestive. The sun has power to melt the snow; and in the meadows all the knolls are bare, and the sheep are gnawing them industriously. The drifts on the side-hills also begin to have a worn and dirty look, and, where they cross the highway, to become soft, letting the

teams in up to their bellies. The oxen labor and grunt, or patiently wait for the shovel to release them; but the spirited horse leaps and flounders, and is determined not to give up. In the woods the snow is melted around the trees, and the burrs and pieces of bark have absorbed the heat till they have sunk half way through to the ground. The snow is melting on the under side; the frost is going out of the ground: now comes the trial of your foundations.

About the farm buildings there awakens the old familiar chorus, the bleating of calves and lambs, and the answering bass of their distressed mothers; while the hens are cackling in the hay-loft, and the geese are noisy in the spring run. But the most delightful of all farm work, or of all rural occupations, is at hand, namely, sugar-making. In New York and northern New England the beginning of this season varies from the first to the middle of March, sometimes even holding off till April. The moment the contest between the sun and frost fairly begins, sugar weather begins; and the more even the contest, the more the sweet. I do not know what the philosophy of it is, but it seems a kind of see-saw, as if the sun drew the sap up and the frost drew it down; and an excess of either stops the flow. Before the sun has got power to unlock the frost, there is no sap; and after the frost has lost its power to lock up again the work of the sun, there is no sap. But when it freezes soundly at night, with a bright, warm sun next day, wind in

the west, and no signs of a storm, the veins of the maples fairly thrill. Pierce the bark anywhere, and out gushes the clear, sweet liquid. But let the wind change to the south and blow moist and warm, destroying that crispness of the air, and the flow slackens at once, unless there be a deep snow in the woods to counteract or neutralize the warmth, in which case the run may continue till the rain sets in. The rough-coated old trees, — one would not think they could scent a change so quickly through that wrapper of dead, dry bark an inch or more thick. I have to wait till I put my head out of doors, and feel the air on my bare cheek, and sniff it with my nose; but their nerves of taste and smell are no doubt under ground, imbedded in the moisture, and if there is anything that responds quickly to atmospheric changes it is water. Do not the fish, think you, down deep in the streams, feel every wind that blows, whether it be hot or cold ? Do not the frogs and newts and turtles under the mud feel the warmth, though the water still seems like ice? As the springs begin to rise in advance of the rain, so the intelligence of every change seems to travel ahead under ground and forewarn things.

A "sap-run" seldom lasts more than two or three days. By that time there is a change in the weather, perhaps a rainstorm, which takes the frost nearly all out of the ground. Then, before there can be another run, the trees must be wound up again, the storm must have a white tail, and "come off" cold. Presently the sun rises clear again, and

cuts the snow or softens the hard-frozen ground with his beams, and the trees take a fresh start. The boys go through the wood, emptying out the buckets or the pans, and reclaiming those that have blown away, and the delightful work is resumed. But the first run, like first love, is always the best, always the fullest, always the sweetest; while there is a purity and delicacy of flavor about the sugpr that far surpasses any subsequent yield.

Trees differ much in the quantity as well as in the quality of sap produced in a given season. Indeed, in a bush or orchard of fifty or one hundred trees, as wide a difference may be observed in this respect as among that number of cows in regard to the milk they yield. I have in my mind now a "sugar-bush'* nestled in the lap of a spur of the Catskills, every tree of which is known to me, and assumes a distinct individuality in my thought. I know the look and quality of the whole two hundred ; and when on my annual visit to the old homestead I find one has perished, or fallen before the axe, I feel a personal loss. They are all veterans, and have yielded up their life's blood for the profit of two or three generations. They stand in little groups or couples. One stands at the head of a spring run, and lifts a large dry branch high above the woods, where hawks and crows love to alight. Half a dozen are climbing a little hill; while others stand far out in the field, as if they had come out to get the sun. A file of five or six worthies sentry the woods on the northwest, and confront a steep

side-hill where sheep and cattle graze. An equal number crowd up to the line on the east; and their gray, stately trunks are seen across meadows or fields of grain. Then there is a pair of Siamese twins, with heavy, bushy tops; while in the forks of a wood-road stand the two brothers, with their arms around each other's neck, and their bodies in gentle contact for a distance of thirty feet.

One immense maple, known as the "old-cream-pan-tree," stands, or did stand, quite alone among a thick growth of birches and beeches. But it kept its end up, and did the work of two or three ordinary trees, as its name denotes. Next to it the best milcher in the lot was a shaggy-barked tree in the edge of the field, that must have been badly crushed or broken when it was little, for it had an ugly crook near the ground, and seemed to struggle all the way up to get in an upright attitude, but never quite succeeded; yet it could outrun all its neighbors nevertheless. The poorest tree in the lot was a short-bodied, heavy-topped tree that stood in the edge of a spring-run. It seldom produced half a gallon of sap during the whole season; but this half gallon was very sweet, — three or four times as sweet as the ordinary article. In the production of sap, top seems far less important than body. It is not length of limb that wins in this race, but length of trunk. A heavy, bushy-topped tree in the open field, for instance, will not, according to my observation, compare with a tall, long-trunked tree in the woods, that has but a small top. Young, thrifty,

thin-skinned trees start up with great spirit, indeed, fairly on a run; but they do not hold out, and their blood is very diluted. Cattle are very fond of sap; so are sheep, and will drink enough to kill them. The honey-bees get here their first sweet, and the earliest bug takes up his permanent abode on the "spile." The squirrels also come timidly down the trees, and sip the sweet flow; and occasionally an ugly lizard, just out of its winter quarters and in quest of novelties, creeps up into the pan or bucket. Soft maple makes a very fine white sugar, superior in quality, but far less in quantity.

I think any person who has tried it will agree with me about the charm of sugar-making, though he have no tooth for the sweet itself. It is enough that it is the first spring work, and takes one to the woods. The robins are just arriving, and their merry calls ring through the glades. The squirrels are now venturing out, and the woodpeckers and nuthatches run briskly up the trees. The crow begins to caw, with his accustomed heartiness and assurance; and one sees the white rump and golden shafts of the high-hole as he flits about the open woods. Next week, or the week after, it may be time to begin plowing, and other sober work about the farm; but this week we will picnic among the maples, and our camp-fire shall be an incense to spring. Ah, I am there now! I see the woods flooded with sunlight; I smell the dry leaves, and the mould under them just quickened by the warmth; the long-trunked maples in their gray, rough liveries

stand thickly aliout; I see the brimming pans and buckets, always on the sunny side of the trees, and hear the musical dropping of the sap; the "boiling-place," with its delightful camp features, is just beyond the first line, with its great arch looking to the southwest. The sound of its axe rings through the woods. Its huge kettles or broad pans boil and foam; and I ask no other delight than to watch and tend them all day, to dip the sap from the great casks into them, and to replenish the fire with the newly-cut birch and beech wood. A slight breeze is blowing from the west; I catch the glint here and there in the afternoon sun of the little rills and creeks coursing down the sides of the hills; the awakening sounds about the farm and the woods reach my ear; and every rustle or movement of the air or on the earth seems like a pulse of returning life in nature. I sympathize with that verdant Hibernian who liked sugar-making so well that he thought he should follow it the whole year. I should at least be tempted to follow the season up the mountains, camping this week on one terrace, next week on one farther up, keeping just on the hem of Winter's garment, and just in advance of the swelling buds, until my smoke went up through the last growth of maple that surrounds the summit. Maple sugar is peculiarly an American product, the discovery of it dating back into the early history of Kew England. The first settlers usually caught the sap in rude troughs, and boiled it down in kettles slung to a pole by a chain, the fire being built

around them. The first step in the way of improvement was to use tin pans instead of troughs, and a large stone arch in which the kettles or caldrons were set with the fire beneath them. But of late years, as the question of fuel has become a more important one, greater improvements have been made. The arch has given place to an immense stove designed for that special purpose; and the kettles to broad, shallow, sheet-iron pans, the object being to economize all the heat, and to obtain the greatest possible extent of evaporating surface.

March 15. — From the first to the middle of March the season made steady progress. There were no checks, no drawbacks. Warm, copious rains from the south and southwest, followed by days of unbroken sunshine. In the moist places — and what places are not moist at this season ? — the sod buzzed like a hive. The absorption and filtration among the network of roots was an audible process.

The clod fairly sang. How the trees responded also! The silver poplars were masses of soft gray bloom, and the willows down toward the river seemed to have slipped off their old bark and on their new in a single night. The soft maples, too, when massed in the distance, their tops deeply dyed in a bright maroon color, — how fair they looked!

The 15th of the month was " one of those charmed days when the genius of God doth flow." The wind died away by mid-forenoon, and the day settled down so softly and lovingly upon the earth,

touching everything, filling everything. The sky visibly came down. You could see it among the trees and between the hills. The sun poured himself into the earth as into a cup, and the atmosphere fairly swam with warmth and light. In the afternoon I walked out over the country roads north of the city. Innumerable columns of smoke were going up all around the horizon from burning brush and weeds, fields being purified by fire. The farmers were hauling out manure; and I am free to confess, the odor of it, with its associations of the farm and the stable, of cattle and horses, was good in my nostrils. In the woods the liverleaf and arbutus had just opened doubtingly; and in the little pools great masses of frogs' spawn, with a milky tinge, were deposited. The youth who accompanied me brought some of it home in his handkerchief, to see it hatch in a goblet.

The month came in like a lamb, and went out like a lamb, setting at naught the old adage. The white fleecy clouds lay here and there, as if at rest, on the blue sky. The fields were a perfect emerald; and the lawns, with the new gold of the first dandelions sprinkled about, were lush with grass. In the parks and groves there was a faint mist of foliage, except among the willows, where there was not only a mist, but a perfect fountain-fall of green. In the distance the river looked blue; the spring freshets at last over; and the ground settled, and the jocund season steps forth into April with a bright Mid confident look.

AUTUMN TIDES

npHE season is always a little behind the sun in our climate, just as the tide is always a little behind the moon. According to the calendar, the summer ought to culminate about the 21st of June, but in reality it is some weeks later; June is a maiden month all through. It is not high noon in nature till about the first or second week in July. When the chestnut-tree blooms, the meridian of the year is reached. By the first of August it is fairly one o'clock. The lustre of the season begins to dim, the foliage of the trees and woods to tarnish, the plumage of the birds to fade, and their songs to cease. The hints of approaching fall are on every hand. How suggestive this thistle-down, for instance, which, as I sit by the open window, comes in and brushes softly across my hand! The first snowfiake tells of winter not more plainly than this driving down heralds the approach of fall. Come here, my fairy, and tell me whence you come and whither you go? What brings you to port here, you gossamer ship sailing the great sea? How exquisitely frail and delicate! One of the lightest things in nature; so light that in the closed room

here it will hardly rest in my open palm. A feather is a clod beside it. Only a spider's web will hold it; coarser objects have no power over it. Caught in the upper currents of the air and rising above the clouds, it might sail perpetually. Indeed, one fancies it might almost traverse the interstellar ether and drive against the stars. And every thistle-head by the roadside holds hundreds of these sky rovers, — imprisoned Ariels unable to set themselves free. Their liberation may be by the shock of the wind, or the rude contact of cattle, but it is oftefter the work of the goldfinch with its complaining brood. The seed of the thistle is the proper food of this bird, and in obtaining it myriads of these winged creatures are scattered to the breeze. Each one is fraught with a seed which it exists to sow, but its wild careering and soaring does not fairly begin till its burden is dropped, and its spheral form is complete. The seeds of many plants and trees are disseminated through the agency of birds; but the thistle furnishes its own birds, — flocks of them, with wings more ethereal and tireless than were ever given to mortal creature. From the pains Nature thus takes to sow the thistle broadcast over the land, it might be expected to be one of the most troublesome and abundant of weeds. But such is not the case; the more pernicious and baffling weeds, like snapdragon or blind nettles, being more local and restricted in their habits, and unable to fly at all.

In the fall, the battles of the spring are fought

over again, beginning at the other or little end of the series. There is the same advance and retreat, with many feints and alarms, between the contending forces, that was witnessed in April and May. The spring comes like a tide running against a strong wind; it is ever beaten back, but ever gaining ground, with now and then a mad "push upon the land" as if to overcome its antagonist at one blow. The cold from the north encroaches upon us in about the same fashion. In September or early in October it usually makes a big stride forward and blackens all the more delicate plants, and hastens the " mortal ripening" of the foliage of the trees, but it is presently beaten back again and the genial warmth repossesses the land. Before long, however, the cold returns to the charge with augmented forces and gains much ground.

The course of the seasons never does run smooth, owing to the unequal distribution of land and water, mountain, wood, and plain.

An equilibrium, however, is usually reached in our climate in October, sometimes the most marked in November, forming the delicious Indian summer; a truce is declared, and both forces, heat and cold, meet and mingle in friendly converse on the field. In the earlier season, this poise of the temperature, this slack-water in nature, comes in May and June; but the October calm is most marked. Day after day, and sometimes week after week, you cannot tell which way the current is setting. Indeed, there is no current, but the season seems to drift a little this

way or a little that, just as the breeze happens to freshen a little in one quarter or the other. The fall of '74 was the most remarkable in this respect I remember ever to have seen. The equilibrium of the season lasted from the middle of October till near December, with scarcely a break. There were six weeks of Indian summer, all gold by day, and, when the moon came, all silver by night. The river was so smooth at times as to be almost invisible, and in its place was the indefinite continuation of the opposite shore down toward the nether world. One seemed to be in an enchanted land, and to breathe all day the atmosphere of fable and romance. Not a smoke, but a kind of shining nimbus filled all the spaces. The vessels would drift by as if in midair with all their sails set. The gypsy blood in one, as Lowell calls it, could hardly stay between four walls and see such days go by. Living in tents, in groves and on the hills, seemed the only natural life.

Late in December we had glimpses of the same weather, —the earth had not yet passed all the golden isles. On the 27th of that month, I find I made this entry in my note-book: "A soft, hazy day, the year asleep and dreaming of the Indian summer again. Not a breath of air and not a ripple on the river. The sunshine is hot as it falls across my table."

But what a terrible winter followed! what a savage chief the fair Indian maiden gave birth to!

This halcyon period of our autumn will always in

some way be associated with the Indian. It is red and yellow and dusky like him. The smoke of his camp-fire seems again in the air. The memory of him pervades the woods. His plumes and moccasins and blanket of skins form just the costume the season demands. It was doubtless his chosen period. The gods smiled upon him then if ever. The time of the chase, the season of the buck and the doe, and of the ripening of all forest fruits; the time when all men are incipient hunters, when the first frosts have given pungency to the air, when to be abroad on the hills or in the woods is a delight that both old and young feel, — if the red aborigine ever had his summer of fullness and contentment, it must have been at this season, and it fitly bears his name.

In how many respects fall imitates or parodies the spring! It is indeed, in some of its features, a sort of second youth of the year. Things emerge and become conspicuous again. The trees attract all eyes as in May. The birds come forth from their summer privacy and parody their spring reunions and rivalries; some of them sing a little after a silence of months. The robins, bluebirds, meadow-larks, sparrows, crows, all sport, and call, and behave in a manner suggestive of spring. The cock grouse drums in the woods as he did in April and May. The pigeons reappear, and the wild geese and ducks. The witch-hazel blooms. The trout spawns. The streams are again full. The air is humid, and the moisture rises in the ground. Na-

ture is breaking camp, as in spring she was going into camp. The spring yearning and restlessness is represented in one by the increased desire to travel.

Spring is the inspiration, fall the expiration. Both seasons have their equinoxes, both their filmy, hazy air, their ruddy forest tints, their cold rains, their drenching fogs, their mystic moons; both have the same solar light and warmth, the same rays of the sun; yet, after all, how different the feelings which they inspire! One is the morning, the other the evening; one is youth, the other is age.

The difference is not merely in us; there is a subtle difference in the air, and in the influences that emanate upon us from the dumb forms of nature. All the senses report a difference. The sun seems to have burned out. One recalls the notion of Herodotus that he is grown feeble, and retreats to the south because he can no longer face the cold and the storms from the north. There is a growing potency about his beams in spring, a waning splendor about them in fall. One is the kindling fire, the other the subsiding flame.

It is rarely that an artist succeeds in painting unmistakably the difference between sunrise and sunset; and it is equally a trial of his skill to put upon canvas the difference between early spring and late fall, say between April and November. It was long ago observed that the shadows are more opaque in the morning than in the evening; the struggle between the light and the darkness more

marked, the gloom more solid, the contrasts more sharp, etc. The rays of the morning sun chisel out and cut down the shadows in a way those of the setting sun do not. Then the sunlight is whiter and newer in the morning, — not so yellow and diffused. A difference akin to this is true of the two seasons I am speaking of. The spring is the morning sunlight, clear and determined; the autumn, the afternoon rays, pensive, lessening, golden.

Does not the human frame yield to and sympathize with the seasons? Are there not more births in the spring and more deaths in the fall? In the spring one vegetates; his thoughts turn to sap; another kind of activity seizes him; he makes new wood which does not harden till past midsummer. For my part, I find all literary work irksome from April to August; my sympathies run in other channels; the grass grows where meditation walked. As fall approaches, the currents mount to the head again. But my thoughts do not ripen well till after there has been a frost. The burrs will not open much before that. A man's thinking, I take it, is a kind of combustion, as is the ripening of fruits and leaves, and he wants plenty of oxygen in the air.

Then the earth seems to have become a positive magnet in the fall; the forge and anvil of the sun have had their effect. In the spring it is negative to all intellectual conditions, and drains one of his lightning.

To-day, October 21st, I found the air in the

bushy fields and lanes under the woods loaded with the perfume of the witch-hazel, —a sweetish, sickening odor. With the blooming of this bush. Nature says, "Positively the last." It is a kind of birth in death, of spring in fall, that impresses one as a little uncanny. All trees and shrubs form their flower-buds in the fall, and keep the secret till spring. How comes the witch-hazel to be the one exception, and to celebrate its floral nuptials on the funeral day of its foliage?

No doubt it will be found that the spirit of some lovelorn squaw has passed into this bush, and that this is why it blooms in the Indian summer rather than in the white man's spring.

But it makes the floral series of the woods complete. Between it and the shad-blow of earliest spring lies the mountain of bloom; the latter at the base on one side, this at the base on the other, with the chestnut blossoms at the top in midsummer.

A peculiar feature of our fall may sometimes be seen of a clear afternoon late in the season. Looking athwart the fields under the sinking sun, the ground appears covered with a shining veil of gossamer. A fairy net, invisible at midday and which the position of the sun now reveals, rests upon the stubble and upon the spears of grass, covering acres in extent, — the work of innumerable little spiders. The cattle walk through it, but do not seem to break it. Perhaps a fly would make his mark upon it. At the same time, stretching from the tops of the trees, or from the top of a stake in the

fence, and leading off toward the sky, may be seen the cables of the flying spider, — a fairy bridge from the visible to the invisible. Occasionally seen against a deep mass of shadow, and perhaps enlarged by clinging particles of dust, they show quite plainly and sag down like a stretched rope, or sway and undulate like a hawser in the tide.

They recall a verse of our rugged poet, Walt Whitman: —

"A noiseless patient spider, I mark'd where, in a little promontory, it stood isolated: Mark'd how, to explore the vacant, vast surrounding. It launch'd forth filament, filament, filament out of itself ; Ever unreeling them —ever tirelessly spreading them.

" And you, 0 my soul, where you stand. Surrounded, surrounded, in measureless oceans of space, Ceaselessly musing, venturing, throwing, — Seeking the spheres to connect them; Till the bridge j-'ou will need be formed — till the ductile anchor hold; Till the gossamer thread you fling, catch somewhere, 0 ray soul."

To return a little, September may be described as the month of tall weeds. Where they have been suffered to stand, along fences, by roadsides, and in forgotten corners, — redroot, pigweed, ragweed, vervain, goldenrod, burdock, elecampane, thistles, teasels, nettles, asters, etc., — how they lift themselves up as if not afraid to be seen now! They are all outlaws; every man's hand is against them; yet how surely they hold their own! They love the roadside, because here they are comparatively safe; and ragged and dusty, like the common

tramps that they are, they form one of the characteristic features of early fall.

I have often noticed in what haste certain weeds are at times to produce their seeds. E-edroot will grow three or four feet high when it has the whole season before it; but let it get a late start, let it come up in August, and it scarcely gets above the ground before it heads out, and apparently goes to work with all its might and main to mature its seed. In the growth of most plants or weeds, April and May represent their root, June and July their stalk, and August and September their flower and seed. Hence, when the stalk months are stricken out, as in the present case, there is only time for a shallow root and a foreshortened head. I think most weeds that get a late start show this curtailment of stalk, and this solicitude to reproduce themselves. But I have not observed that any of the cereals are so worldly wise. They have not had to think and shift for themselves as the weeds have. It does indeed look like a kind of forethought in the redroot. It is killed by the first frost, and hence knows the danger of delay.

How rich in color, before the big show of the tree foliage has commenced, our roadsides are in places in early autumn, — rich to the eye that goes hurriedly by and does not look too closely, — with the profusion of goldenrod and blue and purple asters dashed in upon here and there with the crimson leaves of the dwarf sumac; and at intervals, rising out of the fence corner or crowning a ledge

of rocks, the dark green of the cedars with the still fire of the woodbine at its heart. I wonder if the waysides of other lands present any analogous spectacles at this season.

Then, when the maples have burst out into color, showing like great bonfires along the hills, there is indeed a feast for the eye. A maple before your windows in October, when the sun shines upon it, will make up for a good deal of the light it has excluded; it fills the room with a soft golden glow.

Thoreau, I believe, was the first to remark upon the individuality of trees of the same species with respect to their foliage, — some maples ripening their leaves early and some late, and some being of one tint and some of another; and, moreover, that each tree held to the same characteristics, year after year. There is, indeed, as great a variety among the maples as among the trees of an apple orchard; some are harvest apples, some are fall apples, and some are winter apples, each with a tint of its own. Those late ripeners are the winter varieties, — the Rhode Island greenings or swaars of their kind. The red maple is the early astrachan. Then come the red-streak, the yellow-sweet, and others. There are windfalls among them, too, as among the apples, and one side or hemisphere of the leaf is usually brighter than the other.

The ash has been less noticed for its autumnal foliage than it deserves. The richest shades of plum-color to be seen — becoming by and by, or in certain lights, a deep maroon — are afforded by this

tree. Then at a distance there seems to be sort of bloom on it, as upon the grape or plum. Amid a grove of yellow maple, it makes a most pleasing contrast.

By mid-October, most of the Rip Van Winkles among our brute creatures have lain down for their winter nap. The toads and turtles have buried themselves in the earth. The woodchuck is in his hibernaculum, the skunk in his, the mole in his; and the black bear has his selected, and will go in when the snow comes. He does not like the looks of his big tracks in the snow. They publish his goings and comings too plainly. The coon retires about the same time. The provident wood-mice and the chipmunk are laying by a winter supply of nuts or grain, the former usually in decayed trees, the latter in the ground. I have observed that any unusual disturbance in the woods, near where the chipmunk has his den, will cause him to shift his quarters. One October, for many successive days, I saw one carrying into his hole buckwheat which he had stolen from a near field. The hole was only a few rods from where we were getting out stone, and as our work progressed, and the racket and uproar increased, the chipmunk became alarmed. He ceased carrying in, and after much hesitating and darting about, and some prolonged absences, he began to carry out; he had determined to move; if the mountain fell, he, at least, would be away in time. So, by mouthfuls or cheekfuls, the grain was transferred to a new place. He did not make

a "bee" to get it done, but carried it all himself, occupying several days, and making a trip about every ten minutes.

The red and gray squirrels do not lay by winter stores; their cheeks are made without pockets, and whatever they transport is carried in the teeth. They are more or less active all winter, but October and November are their festal months. Invade some butternut or hickory-nut grove on a frosty October morning, and hear the red squirrel beat the " juba " on a horizontal branch. It is a most lively jig, what the boys call a "regular break-down," interspersed with squeals and snickers and derisive laughter. The most noticeable peculiarity about the vocal part of it is the fact that it is a kind of duet. In other words, by some ventriloquial tricks, he appears to accompany himself, as if his voice split up, a part forming a low guttural sound, and a part a shrill nasal sound.

The distant bark of the more wary gray squirrel may be heard about the same time. There is a teasing and ironical tone in it also, but the gray squirrel is not the Puck the red is.

Insects also go into winter-quarters by or before this time; the bumble-bee, hornet, and wasp. But here only royalty escapes; the queen-mother alone foresees the night of winter coming and the morning of spring beyond. The rest of the tribe try gypsy-ing for a while, but perish in the first frosts. The present October I surprised the queen of the yellow-jackets in the woods looking out a suitable retreat.

The royal dame was house-hunting, and, on being disturbed by my inquisitive poking among the leaves, she got up and flew away with a slow, deep hum. Her body was unusually distended, whether with fat or eggs I am unable to say. In September I took down the nest of the black hornet and found several large queens in it, but the workers had all gone. The queens were evidently weathering the first frosts and storms here, and waiting for the Indian summer to go forth and seek a permanent winter abode. If the covers could be taken off the fields and woods at this season, how many interesting facts of natural history would be revealed! — the crickets, ants, bees, reptiles, animals, and, for aught I know, the spiders and flies asleep or getting ready to sleep in their winter dormitories; the fires of life banked up, and burning just enough to keep the spark over till spring.

The fish all run down the stream in the fall except the trout; it runs up or stays up and spawns in November, the male becoming as brilliantly tinted as the deepest-dyed maple leaf. I have often wondered why the trout spawns in the fall, instead of in the spring like other fish. Is it not because a full supply of clear spring water can be counted on at that season more than at any other? The brooks are not so liable to be suddenly muddied by heavy showers, and defiled with the washings of the roads and fields, as they are in spring and summer. The artificial breeder finds that absolute purity of water is necessary to hatch the spawn; also that shade and a low temperature are indispensable.

Our Northern November day itself is like spring water. It is melted frost, dissolved snow. There is a chill in it and an exhilaration also. The forenoon is all morning and the afternoon all evening. The shadows seem to come forth and to revenge themselves upon the day. The sunlight is diluted with darkness. The colors fade from the landscape, and only the sheen of the river lights up the gray and brown distance.

THE APPLE

Lo! sweetened with the summer light, The full-juiced apple, waxing over-mellow. Drops in silent autumn night.

Tennyson.

ROT a little of the sunshine of our Northern winters is surely wrapped up in the apple. How could we winter over without it! How is life sweetened by its mild acids! A cellar well filled with apples is more valuable than a chamber filled with flax and wool. So much sound, ruddy life to draw upon, to strike one's roots down into, as it were.

Especially to those whose soil of life is inclined to be a little clayey and heavy, is the apple a winter necessity. It is the natural antidote of most of the ills the flesh is heir to. Full of vegetable acids and aromatics, qualities which act as refrigerants and antiseptics, what an enemy it is to jaundice, indigestion, torpidity of liver, etc.! It is a gentle spur and tonic to the whole biliary system. Then I have read that it has been found by analysis to contain more phosphorus than any other vegetable. This makes it the proper food of the scholar and the sedentary man; it feeds his brain and it stimu-

lates his liver. Neither is this all. Beside its hygienic properties, the apple is full of sugar and mucilage, which make it highly nutritious. It is said "the operators of Cornwall, England, consider ripe apples nearly as nourishing as hread, and far more so than potatoes. In the year 1801 — which was a year of much scarcity — apples, instead of being converted into cider, were sold to the poor, and the laborers asserted that they could ' stand their work' on baked apples without meat; whereas a potato diet required either meat or some other substantial nutriment. The French and Germans use apples extensively; so do the inhabitants of all European nations. The laborers depend upon them as an article of food, and frequently make a dinner of sliced apples and bread."

Yet the English apple is a tame and insipid affair, compared with the intense, sun-colored, and sun-steeped fruit our orchards yield. The English have no sweet apple, I am told, the saccharine element apparently being less abundant in vegetable nature in that sour and chilly climate than in our own.

It is well known that the European maple yields no sugar, while both our birch and hickory have sweet in their veins. Perhaps this fact accounts for our excessive love of sweets, which may be said to be a national trait.

The Eussian apple has a lovely complexion, smooth and transparent, but the Cossack is not yet all eliminated from it. The only one I have seen — the Duchess of Oldenburg — is as beautiful as a

Tartar princess,. with a distracting odor, but it is the least bit puckery to the taste.

The best thing I know about Chili is, not its guano beds, but this fact which I learn from Darwin's "Voyage," namely, that the apple thrives well there. Darwin saw a town there so completely buried in a wood of apple-trees, that its streets were merely paths in an orchard. The-tree, indeed, thrives so well, that large branches cut off in the spring and planted two or three feet deep in the ground send out roots and develop into fine, full-bearing trees by the third year. The people know the value of the apple, too. They make cider and wine of it, and then from the refuse a white and finely flavored spirit; then, by another process, a sweet treacle is obtained, called honey. The children and pigs ate little or no other food. He does not add that the people are healthy and temperate, but I have no doubt they are. We knew the apple had many virtues, but these Chilians have really opened a deep beneath a deep. We had found out the cider and the spirits, but who guessed the wine and the honey, except it were the bees ? There is a variety in our orchards called the winesap, a doubly liquid name that suggests what might be done with this fruit.

The apple is the commonest and yet the most varied and beautiful of fruits. A dish of them is as becoming to the centre-table in winter as was the vase of flowers in the summer, — a bouquet of spit--zenburgs and greenings and northern spies. A

rose when it blooms, the apple is a rose when it ripens. It pleases every sense to which it can be addressed, the touch, the smell, the sight, the taste; and when it falls, in the still October days, it pleases the ear. It is a call to a banquet, it is a signal that the'feast is ready. The bough would fain hold it, but it can now assert its independence; it can now live a life of its own.

Daily the stem relaxes its hold, till finally it lets go completely and down comes the painted sphere with a mellow thump to the earth, toward which it has been nodding so long. It bounds away to seek its bed, to hide under a leaf, or in a tuft of grass. It will now take time to meditate and ripen! What delicious thoughts it has there nestled with its fellows under the fence, turning acid into sugar, and sugar into wine!

How pleasing to the touch! I love to stroke its polished rondure with my hand, to carry it in my pocket on my tramp over the winter hills, or through the early spring woods. You are company, you red-cheeked spitz, or you salmon-fleshed greening! I toy with you; press your face to mine, toss you in the air, roll you on the ground, see you shine out where you lie amid the moss and dry leaves and sticks. You are so alive! You glow like a ruddy flower. You look so animated I almost expect to see you move! I postpone the eating of you, you are so beautiful! How compact; how exquisitely tinted! Stained by the sun and varnished against the rains. An independent vegetable existence.

alive and vascular as my own flesh; capable of being wounded, bleeding, wasting away, or almost repairing damages!

How they resist the cold! holding out almost as long as the red cheeks of the boys do. A frost that destroys the potatoes and other roots only makes the apple more crisp and vigorous; they peep out from the chance November snows unscathed. When I see the fruit-vender on the street corner stamping his feet and beating his hands to keep them warm, and his naked apples lying exposed to the blasts, I wonder if they do not ache, too, to clap their hands and enliven their circulation. But they can stand it nearly as long as the vender can.

Noble common fruit, best friend of man and most loved by him, following him, like his dog or his cow, wherever he goes! His homestead is not planted till you are planted, your roots intertwine with his; thriving best where he thrives best, loving the limestone and the frost, the plow and the pruning-knife: you are indeed suggestive of hardy, cheerful industry, and a healthy life in the open air. Temperate, chaste fruit! you mean neither luxury nor sloth, neither satiety nor indolence, neither enervating heats nor the frigid zones. Uncloying fruit, — fruit whose best sauce is the open air, whose finest flavors only he whose taste is sharpened by brisk work or walking knows; winter fruit, when the fire of life burns brightest; fruit always a little hyperborean, leaning toward the cold; bracing, subacid, active fruit! I think you must come from the

north, you are so frank and honest, so sturdy and appetizing. You are stocky and homely like the northern races. Your quality is Saxon. Surely the fiery and impetuous south is not akin to thee. Not spices or olives, or the sumptuous liquid fruits, but the grass, the snow, the grains, the coolness, is akin to thee. I think if I could subsist on you, or the like of you, I should never have an intemperate or ignoble thought, never be feverish or despondent. So far as I could absorb or transmute your quality, I should be cheerful, continent, equitable, sweet-blooded, long-lived, and should shed warmth and contentment around.

Is there any other fruit that has so much facial expression as the apple ? What boy does not more than half believe they can see with that single eye of theirs ? Do they not look and nod to him from the bough? The swaar has one look, the rambo another, the spy another. The youth recognizes the seek-no-further, buried beneath a dozen other varieties, the moment he catches a glance of its eye, or the bonny-cheeked Newtown pippin, or the gentle but sharp-nosed gillyflower. He goes to the great bin in the cellar, and sinks his shafts here and there in the garnered wealth of the orchards, mining for his favorites, sometimes coming plump upon them, sometimes catching a glimpse of them to the right or left, or uncovering them as keystones in an arch made up of many varieties.

In the dark he can usually tell them by the sense of touch. There is not only the size and shape,

but there is the texture and polish. Some apples are coarse-grained and some are fine; some are thin-skinned and some are thick. One variety is quick and vigorous beneath the touch, another gentle and yielding. The pinnock has a thick skin with a spongy lining; a bruise in it becomes like a piece of cork. The tallow apple has an unctuous feel, as its name suggests. It sheds water like a duck., What apple is that with a fat curved stem that blends so prettily with its own flesh, — the wine apple ? Some varieties impress me as masculine, —weather-stained, freckled, lasting, and rugged; others are indeed lady apples, fair, delicate, shining, mild-flavored, white-meated, like the egg-drop and lady-finger. The practiced hand knows each kind by the touch.

Do you remember the apple hole in the garden or back of the house, Ben Bolt ? In the fall, after the bins in the cellar had been well stocked, we excavated a circular pit in the Avarm mellow earth, and, covering the bottom with clean rye straw, emptied in basketful after basketful of hardy choice varieties, till there was a tent-shaped mound several feet high of shining variegated fruit. Then, wrapping it about with a thick layer of long rye straw, and tucking it up snug and warm, the mound was covered with a thin coating of earth, a flat stone on the top holding down the straw. As winter set in, another coating of earth was put upon it, with perhaps an overcoat of coarse dry stable manure, and the precious pile was left in silence and darkness till spring. No

marmot, hibernating under ground in his nest of leaves and dry grass, more cosy and warm. No frost, no wet, but fragrant privacy and quiet. Then how the earth tempers and flavors the apples! It draws out all the acrid unripe qualities, and infuses into them a subtle refreshing taste of the soil. Some varieties perish, but the ranker, hardier kinds, like the northern spy, the greening, or the black apple, or the russet, or the pinnock, how they ripen and grow in grace, how the green becomes gold, and the bitter becomes sweet!

As the supply in the bins and barrels gets low and spring approaches, the buried treasures in the garden are remembered. With spade and axe we go out and penetrate through the snow and frozen earth till the inner dressing of straw is laid bare. It is not quite as clear and bright as when -^e placed it there last fall, but the fruit beneath, which the hand soon exposes, is just as bright and far more luscious. Then, as day after day you resort to the hole, and, removing the straw and earth from the opening, thrust your arm into the fragrant pit, you have a better chance than ever before to become acquainted with your favorites by the sense of touch. How you feel for them, reaching to the right and left! Now you have got a Talman sweet; you imagine you can feel that single meridian line that divides it into two hemispheres. Now a greening fills your hand; you feel its fine quality beneath its rough coat. Now you have hooked a swaar, you recognize its full face; now a Vandevere or a King rolls down

from the apex above and you bag it at once. When you were a schoolboy you stowed these away in your pockets, and ate them along the road and at recess, and again at noontime; and they, in a measure, corrected the effects of the cake and pie with which your indulgent mother filled your lunch-basket.

The boy is indeed the true apple-eater, and is not to be questioned how he came by the fruit with which his pockets are filled. It belongs to him, and he may steal it if it cannot be had in any other way. His own juicy flesh craves the juicy flesh of the apple. Sap draws sap. His fruit-eating has little reference to the state of his appetite. Whether he be full of meat or empty of meat, he wants the apple just the same. Before meal or after meal it never comes amiss. The farm-boy munches apples all day long. He has nests of them in the haymow, mellowing, to which he makes frequent visits. Sometimes old Brindle, having access through the open door, smells them out and makes short work of them.

In some countries the custom remains of placing a rosy apple in the hand of the dead, that they may find it when they enter paradise. In northern mythology the giants eat apples to keep off old age.

The apple is indeed the fruit of youth. As we grow old we crave apples less. It is an ominous sign. When you are ashamed to be seen eating them on the street; when you can carry them in your pocket and your hand not constantly find its way to

them; when your neighbor has apples and you have none, and you make no nocturnal visits to his orchard; when your lunch-basket is without them, and you can pass a winter's night by the fireside with no thought of the fruit at your elbow, — then be assured you are no longer a boy, either in heart or in years.

The genuine apple-eater comforts himself with an apple in their season, as others with a pipe or cigar. When he has nothing else to do, or is bored, he eats an apple. While he is waiting for the train he eats an apple, sometimes several of them. When he takes a walk he arms himself with apples. His traveling bag is full of apples. He offers an apple to his companion, and takes one himself. They are his chief solace when on the road. He sows their seed all along the route. He tosses the core from the car window and from the top of the stage-coach. He would, in time, make the land one vast orchard. He dispenses with a knife. He prefers that his teeth shall have the first taste. Then he knows the best flavor is immediately beneath the skin, and that in a pared apple this is lost. If you will stew the apple, he says, instead of baking it, by all means leave the skin on. It improves the color and vastly heightens the flavor of the dish.

The apple is a masculine fruit; hence women are poor apple-eaters. It belongs to the open air, and requires an open-air taste and relish.

I instantly sympathized with that clergyman I read of, who, on pulling out his pocket-handkerchief

in the midst of his discourse, pulled out two houn-cing apples with it that went rolling across the pulpit floor and down the pulpit stairs. These apples were, no doubt, to be eaten after the sermon, on his way home, or to his next appointment. They would take the taste of it out of his mouth. Then, would a minister be apt to grow tiresome with two big apples in his coat-tail pockets? Would he not naturally hasten along to "lastly" and the big apples? If they were the dominie apples, and it was April or May, he certainly would.

How the early settlers prized the apple! When their trees broke down or were split asunder by the storms, the neighbors turned out, the divided tree was put together again and fastened with iron bolts. In some of the oldest orchards one may still occasionally see a large dilapidated tree with the rusty iron bolt yet visible. Poor, sour fruit, too, but sweet in those early pioneer days. My grandfather, who was one of these heroes of the stump, used every fall to make a journey of forty miles for a few apples, which he brought home in a bag on horseback. He frequently started from home by two or three o'clock in the morning, and at one time both himself and his horse were much frightened by the screaming of panthers in a narrow pass in the mountains through which the road led.

Emerson, I believe, has spoken of the apple as the social fruit of New England. Indeed, what a promoter or abettor of social intercourse among our rural population the apple has been, the company

growing more merry and unrestrained as soon as the basket of apples was passed round! When the cider followed, the introduction and good understanding were complete. Then those rural gatherings that enlivened the autumn in the country, known as "apple-cuts," now, alas! nearly obsolete, where so many things were cut and dried besides apples! The larger and more loaded the orchard, the more frequently the invitations went round and the higher the social and convivial spirit ran. Ours is eminently a country of the orchard. Horace Greeley said he had seen no land in which the orchard formed such a prominent feature in the rural and agricultural districts. Nearly every farmhouse in the Eastern and Northern States has its setting or its background of apple-trees, which generally date back to the first settlement of the farm. Indeed, the orchard, more than almost any other thing, tends to soften and humanize the country, and give the place of which it is an adjunct a settled, domestic look. The apple-tree takes the rawness and wild-ness off any scene. On the top of a mountain, or in remote pastures, it sheds the sentiment of home. It never loses its domestic air, or lapses into a wild state. And in planting a homestead, or in choosing a building site for the new house, tvliat a help it is to have a few old, maternal apple-trees near by, — regular old grandmothers, who have seen trouble, who have been sad and glad through so many winters and summers, who have blossomed till the air about them is sweeter than elsewhere, and borne

THE APPLE 125

fruit till the grass beneath them has become thick and soft from human contact, and who have nourished robins and finches in their branches till they have a tender, brooding look! The ground, the turf, the atmosphere of an old orchard, seem several stages nearer to man than that of the adjoining field, as if the trees had given back to the soil more than they had taken from it; as if they had tempered the elements, and attracted all the genial and beneficent influences in the landscape arovmd.

An apple orchard is sure to bear you several crops beside the apple. There is the crop of sweet and tender reminiscences, dating from childhood and spanning the seasons from May to October, and making the orchard a sort of outlying part of the household. You have played there as a child, mused there as a youth or lover, strolled there as a thoughtful, sad-eyed man. Your father, perhaps, planted the trees, or reared them from the seed, and you yourself have pruned and grafted them, and worked among them, till every separate tree has a peculiar history and meaning in your mind. Then there is the never-failing crop of birds, — robins, goldfinches, kingbirds, cedar-birds, hairbirds, orioles, starlings, —all nesting and breeding in its branches, and fitly described by Wilson Flagg as " Birds of the Garden and Orchard." Whether the pippin and sweet bough bear or not, the " punctual birds " can always be depended on. Indeed, there are few better places to study ornithology than in the orchard. Besides its regular occupants, many of

the birds of the deeper forest find occasion to visit it during the season. The cuckoo comes for the tent-caterpillar, the jay for frozen apples, the ruffed grouse for buds, the crow foraging for birds' eggs, the woodpecker and chickadees for their food, and the high-hole for ants. The redbird comes, too, if only to see what a friendly covert its branches form; and the wood thrush now and then comes out of the grove near by, and nests alongside of its cousin, the robin. The smaller hawks know that this is a most likely spot for their prey, and in spring the shy northern warblers jnay be studied as they pause to feed on the fine insects amid its branches. The mice love to dwell here also, and hither come from the near woods the squirrel and the rabbit. The latter will put his head through the boy's slipper-noose any time for a taste of the sweet apple, and the red squirrel and chipmunk esteem its seeds a great rarity.

All the domestic animals love the apple, but none so much so as the cow. The taste of it wakes her up as few other things do, and bars and fences must be well looked after. No need to assort them or pick out the ripe ones for her. An apple is an apple, and there is no best about it. I heard of a quick-witted old cow that learned to shake them down from the tree. While rubbing herself she had observed that an apple sometimes fell. This stimulated her to rub a little harder, when more apples fell. She then took the hint and rubbed her shoulder with such vigor that the farmer had to

check her, and keep an eye on her to save his fruit.

But the cow is the friend of the apple. How many trees she has planted about the farm, in the edge of the woods, and in remote fields and pastures ! The wild apples, celebrated by Thoreau, are mostly of her planting. She browses them down, to be sure, but they are hers, and why should she not?

What an individuality the apple-tree has, each variety being nearly as marked by its form as by its fruit. What a vigorous grower, for instance, is the E-ibston pippin, an English apple, — wide-branching like the oak; its large ridgy fruit, in late fall or early winter, is one of my favorites. Or the thick and more pendent top of the bellflower, with its equally rich, sprightly, uncloying fruit.

Sweet apples are perhaps the most nutritious, and when baked are a feast of themselves. With a tree of the Jersey sweet or of the Talman sweet in bearing, no man's table need be devoid of luxuries and one of the most wholesome of all desserts. Or the red astrachan, an August apple,—what a gap may be filled in the culinary department of a household at this season by a single tree of this fruit! And what a feast is its shining crimson coat to the eye before its snow-white flesh has reached the tongue! But the apple of apples for the household is the spitzenburg. In this casket Pomona has put her highest flavors. It can stand the ordeal of cooking, and still remain a spitz. I recently saw a barrel of these apples from the orchard of a fruit-grower in the northern part of New York, who has devoted especial attention to this variety. They were perfect gems. Not large,— that had not been the aim, — but small, fair, uniform, and red to the core. How intense, how spicy and aromatic!

But all the excellences of the apple are not confined to the cultivated fruit. Occasionally a seedling springs up about the farm that produces fruit of rare beauty and worth. In sections peculiarly adapted to the apple, like a certain belt along the Hudson River, I have noticed that most of the wild, unbidden trees bear good, edible fruit. In cold and ungenial districts the seedlings are mostly sour and crabbed, but in more favorable soils they are oftener mild and sweet. I know wild apples that ripen in August, and that do not need, if it could be had, Thoreau's sauce of sharp, November air to be eaten with. At the foot of a hill near me, and striking its roots deep in the shale, is a giant specimen of native tree that bears an apple that has about the clearest, waxiest, most transparent complexion I ever saw. It is of good size, and the color of a tea rose. Its quality is best appreciated in the kitchen. I know another seedling of excellent quality, and so remarkable for its firmness and density that it is known on the farm where it grows as the "heavy apple."

I have alluded to Thoreau, to whom all lovers of the apple and its tree are under obligation. His chapter on Wild Apples is a most delicious piece of writing. It has.a "tang and smack" like the fruit it celebrates, and is dashed and streaked with color in the same manner. It has the hue and perfume of the crab, and the richness and raciness of the pippin. But Thoreau loved other apples than the wild sorts, and was obliged to confess that his favorites could not be eaten indoors. Late in November he found a blue-pearmain tree growing within the edge of a swamp, almost as good as wild. " You would not suppose," he says, "that there was any fruit left there on the first survey, but you must look according to system. Those which lie exposed are quite brown and rotten now, or perchance a few still show one blooming cheek here and there amid the wet leaves. Nevertheless, with experienced eyes I explore amid the bare alders, and the huckleberry bushes, and the withered sedge, and in the crevices of the rocks, which are full of leaves, and pry under the fallen and decaying ferns which, with apple and alder leaves, thickly strew the ground. For I know that they lie concealed, fallen into hollows long since, and covered up by the leaves of the tree itself, — a proper kind of packing. From these lurking places, anywhere within the circumference of the tree, I draw forth the fruit all wet and glossy, maybe nibbled by rabbits and hollowed out by crickets, and perhaps with a leaf or two cemented to it (as Curzon an old manuscript from a monastery's mouldy cellar), but still with a rich bloom on it, and at least as ripe and well kept, if not better than those in barrels, more crisp and lively than

they. If these resources fail to yield anything, I have learned to look between the bases of the suckers which spring thickly from some horizontal limb, for now and then one lodges there, or in the very midst of an alder-clump, where they are covered by leaves, safe from cows which may have smelled them out. If I am sharp-set,—for I do not refuse the blue-pearmain,— I fill my pockets on each side; and as I retrace my steps in the frosty eve, being perhaps four or five miles from home, I eat one first from this side, and then from that, to keep my balance."

VITI

AN OCTOBER ABROAD

I

MELLOW ENGLAND

"T WILL say at tlie outset, as I believe some one -^ else has said on a like occasion, that in this narrative I shall probably describe myself more than the objects I look upon. The facts and particulars of the case have already been set down in the guidebooks and in innumerable books of travel. I shall only attempt to give an account of the pleasure and satisfaction I had in coming face to face with things in the mother country, seeing them as I did with kindred and sympathizing eyes.

The ocean was a dread fascination to me, — a world whose dominion I had never entered; but I proved to be such a wretched sailor that I am obliged to confess, Hibernian fashion, that the happiest moment I spent upon the sea was when I set my foot upon the land.

It is a wide and fearful gulf that separates the two worlds. The landsman can know little of the wildness, savageness, and mercilessness of nature till he has been upon the sea. It is as if he had taken a

leap off into the interstellar spaces. In voyaging to Mars or Jupiter, he might cross such a desert,— might confront such awful purity and coldness. An astronomic solitariness and remoteness encompass the sea. The earth and all remembrance of it is blotted out; there is no hint of it anywhere. This is not water, this cold, blue-black, vitreous liquid. It suggests, not life, but death. Indeed, the regians of everlasting ice and snow are not more cold and inhuman than is the sea.

Almost the only thing about my first sea voyage that I remember with pleasure is the circumstance of the little birds that, during the first few days out, took refuge on the steamer. The first afternoon, just as we were losing sight of land, a delicate little wood-bird, the black and white creeping warbler, — having lost its reckoning in making perhaps its first southern voyage, — came aboard. It was much fatigued, and had a disheartened, demoralized look. After an hour or two it disappeared, having, I fear, a hard pull to reach the land in the face of the wind that was blowing, if indeed it reached it at all.

The next day, just at night, I observed a small hawk sailing about conveniently near the vessel, but with a very lofty, independent mien, as if he had just happened that way on his travels, and was only lingering to take a good view of us. It was amusing to observe his coolness and haughty unconcern in that sad plight he was in; by nothing in his manner betraying that he was several hundred miles at sea, and did not know how he was going to get back to land. But presently I noticed he found it not inconsistent with his dignity to alight on the rigging under friendly cover of the tops'l, where I saw his feathers rudely ruffled by the wind, till darkness set in. If the sailors did not disturb him during the night, he certainly needed all his fortitude in the morning to put a cheerful face on his situation.

The third day, when we were perhaps off Nova Scotia or Newfoundland, the American pipit or titlark, from the far north, a brown bird about the size of a sparrow, dropped upon the deck of the ship, so nearly exhausted that one of the sailors was on the point of covering it with his hat. It stayed about the vessel nearly all day, flitting from point to point, or hopping along a few feet in front of the promenaders, and prying into every crack and crevice for food. Time after time I saw it start off with a reassuring chirp, as if determined to seek the land; but before it had got many rods from the ship its heart would seem to fail it, and, after circling about for a few moments, back it would come, more discouraged than ever.

These little waifs from the shore! I gazed upon them with a strange, sad interest. They were friends in distress; but the sea-birds, skimming along indifferent to us, or darting in and out among those watery hills, I seemed to look upon as my natural enemies. They were the nurslings and favorites of the sea, and I had no sympathy with them.

No doubt the number of our land-birds that actually perish in the sea during their autumn migration, being carried far out of their course by the prevailing westerly winds of this season, is very great. Occasionally one makes the passage to Great Britain by following the ships, and finding them at convenient distances along the route; and I have been told that over fifty different species of our more common birds, such as robins, starlings, grosbeaks, thrushes, etc., have been found in Ireland, having, of course, crossed in this way. What numbers of these little navigators of the air are misled and wrecked, during those dark and stormy nights, on the lighthouses alone that line the Atlantic coast? Is it Celia Thaxter who tells of having picked up her apron full of sparrows, warblers, flycatchers, etc., at the foot of the lighthouse on the Isles of Shoals, one morning after a storm, the ground being still strewn with birds of all kinds that had dashed themselves against the beacon, bewildered and fascinated by its tremendous light?

If a land-bird perishes at sea, a sea-bird is equally cast away upon the land; and I have known the sooty tern, with its almost omnipotent wing, to fall down, utterly famished and exhausted, two hundred miles from salt water.

But my interest in these things did not last beyond the third day. About this time we entered what the sailors call the "devil's hole," and a very respectably-sized hole it is, extending from the banks of Newfoundland to Ireland, and in all seasons and weathers it seems to be well stirred up.

Amidst the' tossing and rolling, the groaning of penitent travelers, and the laboring of the vessel as she climbed those dark unstable mountains, my mind reverted feebly to Huxley's statement, that the bottom of this sea, for over a thousand miles, presents to the eye of science a vast chalk plain, over which one might drive as over a floor, and I tried to solace myself by dwelling upon the spectacle of a solitary traveler whipping up his steed across it. The imaginary rattle of his wagon was like the sound of lutes and harps, and I would rather have clung to his-axletree than been rocked in the best berth in the ship.

On the tenth day, about four o'clock in the afternoon, we sighted Ireland. The ship came up from behind the horizon, where for so many days she had been buffeting with the winds and the waves, but had never lost the clew, bearing straight as an arrow for the mark. I think, if she had been aimed at a fair-sized artillery target, she would have crossed the ocean and struck the bull's-eye.

In Ireland, instead of an emerald isle rising out of the sea, I beheld a succession of cold, purplish mountains, stretching along the northeastern horizon, but I am bound to say that no tints of bloom or verdure were ever half so welcome to me as were those dark, heather-clad ranges. It is a feeling which a man can have but once in his life, when he first sets eyes upon a foreign land; and in my case, to this

feeling was added the delightful thought that the "devil's hole" would soon be cleared and my long fast over.

Presently, after the darkness had set in, signal rockets were let off from the stern of the vessel, writing their burning messages upon the night; and when answering rockets rose slowly up far ahead, I suppose we all felt that the voyage was essentially done, and no doubt a message flashed back under the ocean that the Scotia had arrived.

The sight of the land had been such medicine to me that I could now hold up my head and walk about, and so went down for the first time and took a look at the engines, — those twin monsters that had not stopped once, or apparently varied their stroke at all, since leaving Sandy Hook; I felt like patting their enormous cranks and shafts with my hand,—then at the coal bunks, vast cavernous recesses in the belly of the ship, like the chambers of the original mine in the mountains, and saw the men and firemen at work in a sort of purgatory of heat and dust. When it is remembered that one of these ocean steamers consumes about one hundred tons of coal per day, it is easy to imagine what a burden the coal for a voyage alone must be, and one is not at all disposed to laugh at Dr. Lardner, who proved so convincingly that no steamship could ever cross the ocean, because it could not carry coal enough to enable it to make the passage.

On the morrow, a calm lustrous day, we steamed at our leisure up the Channel and across the Irish

Sea, the coast of Wales, and her groups of lofty mountains, in full view nearly all day. The mountains were in profile like the Catskills viewed from the Hudson below, only it was evident there were no trees or shrubbery upon them, and their summits, on this last day of September, were white with the snow.

ASHORE

The first day or half day ashore is, of course, the most novel and exciting; but who, as Mr. Higgin-son says, can describe his sensations and emotions this first half day 1 It is a page of travel that has not yet been written. Paradoxical as it may seem, one generally comes out of pickle much fresher than he went in. The sea has given him an enormous appetite for the land. Every one of his senses is like a hungry wolf clamorous to be fed. For my part, I had suddenly emerged from a condition bordering on that of the hibernating animals — a condition in which I had neither eaten, nor slept, nor thought, nor moved, when I could help it — into not only a full, but a keen and joyous, possession of my health and faculties. It was almost a metamorphosis. I was no longer the clod I had been, but a bird exulting in the earth and air, and in the liberty of motion. Then to remember it was a new earth and a new sky that I was beholding,— that it was England, the old mother at last, no longer a faith or a fable, but an actual fact there before my eyes and under my feet, — why should I not exult? Go to! I will be indulged. These trees, those fields,

that bird darting along the hedge-rows, those men and boys picking blackberries in October, those English flowers by the roadside (stop the carriage while I leap out and pluck them), the homely, domestic looks of things, those houses, those queer vehicles, those thick-coated horses, those big-footed, coarsely-clad, clear-skinned men and women, this massive, homely, compact architecture,— let me have a good look, for this is my first hour in England, and I am drunk with the joy of seeing! This house-fly even, let me inspect it; ^ and that swallow skimming along so familiarly,— is he the same I saw trying to cling to the sails of the vessel the third day out? or is the swallow the swallow the world over 1 This grass I certainly have seen before, and this red and white clover, but this daisy and dandelion are not the same; and I have come three thousand miles to see the mullein cultivated in a garden, and christened the velvet plant.

As we sped through the land, the heart of England, toward London, I thought my eyes would never get their fill of the landscape, and that I would lose them out of my head by their eagerness to catch every object as we rushed along! How they reveled, how they followed the birds and the game, how they glanced ahead on the track — that marvelous track I — or shot ofl* over the fields and downs, finding their delight in the streams, the roads, the bridges, the splendid breeds of cattle and

1 The English house-fly actually seemed coarser and more hairy than ours.

sheep in the fields, the superb husbandry, the rich mellow soil, the drainage, the hedges, — in the in-conspicuousness of any given feature, and the mellow tone and homely sincerity of all; now dwelling fondly upon the groups of neatly modeled stacks, then upon the field occupations, the gathering of turnips and cabbages, or the digging of potatoes, — how I longed to turn up the historic soil, into which had passed the sweat and virtue of so many generations, with my own spade, — then upon the quaint, old, thatched houses, or the cluster of tiled roofs, then catching at a church spire across a meadow (and it is all meadow), or at the remains of tower or wall overrun with ivy.

Here, something almost human looks out at you from the landscape; Nature here has been so long under the dominion of man, has been taken up and laid down by him so many times, worked over and over with his hands, fed and fattened by his toil and industry, and, on the whole, has proved herself •so willing and tractable, that she has taken on something of his image, and seems to radiate his presence. She is completely domesticated, and no doubt loves the titivation of the harrow and plow. The fields look half conscious; and if ever the cattle have "great and tranquil thoughts," as Emerson suggests they do, it must be when lying upon these lawns and meadows. I noticed that the trees, the oaks and elms, looked like fruit-trees, or as if they had felt the humanizing influences of so many generations of men, and were betaking themselves from

the woods to the orchard. The game is more than half tame, and one could easily understand that it had a keeper.

But the look of those fields and parks went straight to my heart. It is not merely that they were so smooth and cultivated, but that they were so benign and maternal, so redolent of cattle and sheep and of patient, homely farm labor. One gets only here and there a glimpse of such in this country. I see occasionally about our farms a patch of an acre or half acre upon which has settled this atmosphere of ripe and loving husbandry; a choice bit of meadow about the barn or orchard, or near the house, which has had some special fattening, perhaps been the site of some former garden, or barn, or homestead, or which has had the wash of some building, where the feet of children have played for generations, and the flocks and herds have been fed in winter, and where they love to lie and ruminate at night, — a piece of sward thick and smooth, and full of warmth and nutriment, where the grass is greenest and freshest in spring, and the hay finest and thickest in summer.

This is the character of the whole of England that I saw. I had been told I should see a garden, but I did not know before to what an extent the earth could become a living repository of the virtues of so many generations of gardeners. The tendency to run to weeds and wild growths seems to have been utterly eradicated from the soil; and if anything were to spring up spontaneously, I think it would be cabbage and turnips, or grass and grain.

And yet, to American eyes, the country seems quite uninhabited, there are so few dwellings and so few people. Such a landscape at home would be dotted all over with thrifty farmhouses, each with its group of painted outbuildings, and along every road and highway would be seen the well-to-do turnouts of the independent freeholders. But in England the dwellings of the poor people, the farmers, are so humble and inconspicuous and are really so far apart, and the halls and the country-seats of the aristocracy are so hidden in the midst of vast estates, that the landscape seems almost deserted, and it is not till you see the towns and great cities that you can. understand where so vast a population keeps itself.

Another thing that would be quite sure to strike my eye on this my first ride across British soil, and on all subsequent rides, was the enormous number of birds and fowls of various kinds that swarmed in the air or covered the ground. It was truly amazing. It seemed as if the feathered life of a whole continent must have been concentrated on this island. Indeed, I doubt if a sweeping together of all the birds of the United States into any tAvo of the largest States would people the earth and air more fully. There appeared to be a plover, a crow, a rook, a blackbird, and a sparrow to every square yard of ground. They know the value of birds in Britain,— that they are the friends, not the enemies, of the farmer. It must be the paradise of crows and rooks. It did me good to see them so much at

home about the fields and even in the towns. I was glad also to see that the British crow was not a stranger to me, and that he differed from his brother on the American side of the Atlantic only in being less alert and cautious, having less use for these qualities.

Now and then the train would start up some more tempting game. A brace or two of partridges or a covey of quails would settle down in the stubble, or a cock pheasant drop head and tail and slide into the copse. Rabbits also would scamper back from the borders of the fields into the thickets or peep slyly out, making my sportsman's fingers tingle.

I have no doubt I should be a notorious poacher in England. How could an American see so much game and not wish to exterminate it entirely as he does at home ? But sporting is an expensive luxury here. In the first place a man pays a heavy tax on his gun, nearly or quite half its value; then he has to have a license to hunt, for which he pays smartly; then permission from the owner of the land upon which he wishes to hunt, so that the game is hedged about by a triple safeguard.

An American, also, will be at once struck with the look of greater substantiality and completeness in everything he sees here. No temporizing, no makeshifts, no evidence of hurry, or failure, or contract work; no wood and little paint, but plenty of iron and brick and stone. This people have taken plenty of time, and have built broad and deep, and placed the cap-stone on. All this I had

been told, but it pleased me so in the seeing that I must tell it again. It is worth a voyage across the Atlantic to see the bridges alone. I believe I had seen little other than wooden bridges before, and in England I saw not one such, but everywhere solid arches of masonry, that were refreshing and reassuring to behold. Even the lanes and byways about the farm, I noticed, crossed the little creeks with a span upon which an elephant would not hesitate to tread, or artillery trains to pass. There is no form so pleasing to look upon as the arch, or that affords so much food and suggestion to the mind. It seems to stimulate the volition, the will-power, and for my part I cannot look upon a noble span without a feeling of envy, for I know the hearts of heroes are thus keyed and fortified. The arch is the symbol of strength and activity, and of rectitude. In Europe I took a new lease of this feeling, this partiality for the span, and had daily opportunities to indulge and confirm it. In London I had immense satisfaction in observing the bridges there, and in walking over them, firm as the geological strata and as enduring. London Bridge, Waterloo Bridge, Blackfriars, etc., clearing the river in a few gigantic leaps, like things of life and motion, — to pass over one of these bridges, or to sail under it, awakens the emotion of the sublime. I think the moral value of such a bridge as the Waterloo must be inestimable. It seems to me the British Empire itself is stronger for such a bridge, and that all public and private virtues are stronger. In Paris, too, those

superb monuments over the Seine, — I think tliey alone ought to inspire the citizens with a love of permanence, and help hold them to stricter notions of law and dependence. No doubt kings and tyrants know the value of these things, and as yet they certainly have the monopoly of them.

LONDON

I am too good a countryman to feel much at home in cities, and usually value them only as conveniences, but for London I conceived quite an affection; perhaps because it is so much like a natural formation itself, and strikes less loudly, or perhaps sharply, upon the senses than our great cities do. It is a forest of brick and stone of the most stupendous dimensions, and one traverses it in the same adventurous kind of way that he does woods and mountains. The maze and tangle of streets is something fearful, and any generalization of them a step not to be hastily taken. My experience heretofore had been that cities generally were fractions that could be greatly reduced, but London I found I could not simplify, and every morning for weeks, when I came out of my hotel, it was a question whether my course lay in this direction or in squarely the opposite. It has no unit of structure, but is a vast aggregation of streets and houses, or in fact of towns and cities, which have to be mastered in detail. I tried the third or fourth day to get a bird's-eye view from the top of St. Paul's, but saw through the rifts in the smoke only a waste, —

literally a waste of red tiles and chimney pots. The confusion and desolation were complete.

But I finally mastered the city, in a measure, by the aid of a shilling map, which I carried with me wherever I went, and upon which when I was lost I would hunt myself up, thus making in the end a very suggestive and entertaining map. Indeed, every.inch of this piece of colored paper is alive to me. If I did not make the map itself, I at least verified it, which is nearly as good, and the verification, on street corner by day and under lamp or by shop window at night, was often a matter of so much concern that I doubt if the original surveyor himself put more heart into certain parts of his work than I did in the proof of them.

London has less metropolitan splendor than New York, and less of the full-blown pride of the shopman. Its stores are not nearly so big, and it has no signboards that contain over one thousand feet of lumber; neither did I see any names painted on the gable ends of the buildings that the man in the moon could read without his opera-glass. I went out one day to look up one of the great publishing houses, and passed it and repassed it several times trying to find the sign. Finally, having made sure of the building, I found the name of the firm cut into the door jamb.

London seems to have been built and peopled by countrymen, who have preserved all the rural reminiscences possible. All its great streets or avenues are called roads, as King's Eoad, City Road, Edge-

ware Road, Tottenham Court Koad, etc., with innumerable lesser roads. Then there are lanes and walks, and such rural names among the streets as Long Acre, Snowhill, Poultry, Bush-lane, Hill-road, Hounsditch, etc., and not one grand street or imperial avenue.

My visit fell at a most favorable juncture as to weather, there being but few rainy days and but little fog. I had imagined that they had barely enough fair weather in London, at any season, to keep alive the tradition of sunshine and of blue sky, but the October days I spent there were not so very far behind what we have at home at this season. London often puts on a nightcap of smoke and fog, which it pulls down over its ears pretty close at times; and the sun has a habit of lying abed very late in the morning, which all the people imitate; but I remember some very pleasant weather there, and some bright moonlight nights.

I saw but one full-blown characteristic London fog. I was in the National Gallery one day, trying to make up my mind about Turner, when this chimney-pot meteor came down. It was like a great yellow dog taking possession of the world. The light faded from the room, the pictures ran together in confused masses of shadow on the walls, and in the street only a dim yellowish twilight prevailed, through which faintly twinkled the lights in the shop windows. Vehicles came slowly out of the dirty obscurity on one side and plunged into it on the other. Waterloo Bridge gave one or two leaps

and disappeared, and the Nelson Column in Trafalgar Square was obliterated for half its length. Travel was impeded, boats stopped on the river, trains stood still on the track, and for an hour and a half London lay buried beneath this sickening eruption. I say eruption, because a London fog is only a London smoke tempered by a moist atmosphere. It is called "fog" by courtesy, but lampblack is its chief ingredient. It is not wet like our fogs, but quite dry, and makes the eyes smart and the nose tingle. Whenever the sun can be seen through it, his face is red and dirty; seen through a bona fide fog, his face is clean and white. English coal — or " coals " as they say here in burning gives out an enormous quantity of thick, yellowish smoke, which is at no time absorbed or dissipated as it would be in our hard, dry atmosphere, and which at certain times is not absorbed at all, but falls down swollen and augmented by the prevailing moisture. The atmosphere of the whole island is more or less impregnated with smoke, even on the fairest days, and it becomes more and more dense as you approach the great towns. Yet this compound of smut, fog, and common air is an elixir of youth; and this is one of the surprises of London, to see amid so much soot and dinginess such fresh, blooming complexions, and in general such a fine physical tone and full-bloodedness among the people, — such as one has come to associate only with the best air and the purest, wholesomest country influences. What the secret of it may be, I am at a loss to know, unless

it is that the moist atmosphere does not dry up the blood as our air does, and that the carbon and creosote have some rare antiseptic and preservative qualities, as doubtless they have, that are efficacious in the human physiology. It is no doubt true, also, that the people do not tan in this climate, as in ours, and that the delicate flesh tints show more on that account.

I speak thus of these things with reference to our standards at home, because I found that these standards were ever present in my mind, and that I was unconsciously applying them to whatever I saw and wherever I went, and often, as I shall have occasion to show, to their discredit.

Climate is a great matter, and no doubt many of the differences between the English stock at home and its offshoot in our country are traceable to this source. Our climate is more heady and less stomachic than the English; sharpens the wit, but dries up the fluids and viscera; favors an irregular, nervous energy, but exhausts the animal spirits. It is, perhaps, on this account that I have felt since my return how much easier it is to be a dyspeptic here than in Great Britain. One's appetite is keener and more ravenous, and the temptation to bolt one's food greater. The American is not so hearty an eater as the Englishman, but the forces of his body are constantly leaving his stomach in the lurch, and running off into his hands and feet and head. His eyes are bigger than his belly, but an Englishman's belly is a deal larger than his eyes,

and the number of plum puddings and amount of Welsh rarebit he devours annually would send the best of us to his grave in half that time. We have not enough constitutional inertia and stolidity; our climate gives us no rest, but goads us day and night; and the consequent wear and tear of life is no doubt greater in this country than in any other on the globe. We are playing the game more rapidly, and I fear less thoroughly and sincerely, than the mother country.

The more uniform good health of English women is thought to be a matter of exercise in the open air, as walking, riding, etc., but the prime reason is mainly a climatic one, uniform habits of exercise being more easily kept up in that climate than in this, and being less exhaustive, one day with another. You can walk there every day in the year without much discomfort, and the stimulus is about the same. Here it is too hot in summer and too cold in winter, or else it keys you up too tight one day and unstrings you the next; all fire and motion in the morning, and all listlessness and ennui in the afternoon; a spur one hour and a sedative the next.

A watch will not keep as steady time here as in Britain, and the human clock-work is more liable to get out of repair for the same reason. Our women, especially, break down prematurely, and the decay of maternity in this country is no doubt greater than in any of the oldest civilized communities. One reason, doubtless, is that our women are the greatest slaves of fashion in the whole world, and, in follow-

ing the whims of that famous courtesan, have the most fickle and destructive climate to contend with.

English women all have good-sized feet, and Englishmen, too, and wear large, comfortable shoes. This was a noticeable feature at once; coarse, loose-fitting clothes of both sexes, and large boots and shoes with low heels. They evidently knew the use of their feet, and had none of the French, or American, or Chinese fastidiousness about this part of their anatomy. I notice that, when a family begins to run out, it turns out its toes, drops off at the heel, shortens its jaw, and dotes on small feet and hands.

Another promoter of health in England is woolen clothes, which are worn the year round, the summer driving people into no such extremities as here. And the good, honest woolen stuff's of one kind and another that fill the shops attest the need and the taste that prevails. They had a garment when I was in London called the Ulster overcoat, — a coarse, shaggy, bungling coat, with a skirt nearly reaching to the feet, very ugly, tried by the fashion plates, but very comfortable, and quite the fashion. This very sensible garment has since become well known in America.

The Americans in London were put out with the tailors, and could rarely get suited, on account of the loose cutting and the want of "style." But "style" is the hiatus that threatens to swallow us all one of these days. About the only monstrosity I saw in the British man's dress was the stove-pipe

hat, which everybody wears. At first I feared it might be a police regulation, or a requirement of the British Constitution, for I seemed to be about the only man in the kingdom with a soft hat on, and I had noticed that before leaving the steamer every man brought out from its hiding-place one of these polished brain-squeezers. Even the boys wear them, — youths of nine and ten years with little stovepipe hats on; and at Eton School I saw black swarms of them:

even the boys in the field were playing football in stove-pipe hats.

What we call beauty in womau is so much a matter of youth and health that the average of female beauty in London is, I believe, higher than in this country. English women are comely and good-looking. It is an extremely fresh and pleasant face that you see everywhere, — softer, less clearly and sharply cut than the typical female face in this country,— less spiriticelle, less perfect in form, but stronger and sweeter. There is more blood, and heart, and substance back of it. The American race of the present generation is doubtless the most shapely, both in face and figure, that has yet appeared. American children are far less crude, and lumpy, and awkward-looking than the European children. One generation in this country suffices vastly to improve the looks of the offspring of the Irish or German or Norwegian emigrant. There is surely something in our climate or conditions that speedily refines and sharpens — and, shall I add, hardens? — the human features. The face loses

something, but it comes into shape; and of such beauty as is the product of this tendency we can undoubtedly show more, especially in our women, than the parent stock in Europe; while American schoolgirls, I believe, have the most bewitching beauty in the world.

The English plainness of speech is observable even in the signs or notices along the streets. Instead of "Lodging," "Lodging," as with us, one sees "Beds," "Beds," which has a very homely sound; and in place of "gentlemen's" this, that, or the other, about public places, the word "men's" is used.

I suppose, if it was not for the bond of a written language and perpetual intercourse, the two nations would not be able to understand each other in the course of a hundred years, the inflection and accentuation is so different. I recently heard an English lady say, referring to the American speech, that she could hardly believe her own language could be spoken so strangely.

ARCHITECTURE

One sees right away that the English are a home people, a domestic people; and he does not need to go into their houses or homes to find this out. It is in the air and in the general aspect of things. Everywhere you see the virtue and quality that we ascribe to home-made articles. It seems as if tilings had been made by hand, and with care and affection, as they have been. The land of caste and kings,

there is yet less glitter and display than in this country, less publicity, and, of course, less rivalry and emulation also, for which we pay very dearly. You have got to where the word homely preserves its true signification, and is no longer a term of dis. paragement, but expressive of a cardinal virtue.

I liked the English habit of naming their houses; it shows the importance they attach to their homes. All about the suburbs of London and in the outlying villages I noticed nearly every house and cottage had some appropriate designation, as Terrace House, Oaktree House, Ivy Cottage, or some Villa, etc., usually cut into the stone gate-post, and this name is put on the address of the letters. How much better to be known by your name than by your number! I believe the same custom prevails in the country, and is common to the middle classes as well as to the aristocracy. It is a good feature. A house or a farm with an appropriate name, which everybody recognizes, must have an added value and importance.

Modern English houses are less showy than ours, and have more weight and permanence,— no flat roofs and no painted outside shutters. Indeed, that pride of American country people, and that abomination in the landscape, a white house with green blinds, I did not see a specimen of in England. They do not aim to make their houses conspicuous, but the contrary. They make a large, yellowish brick that has a pleasing effect in the wall. Then a very short space of time in that climate suffices to

take off the effect of newness, and give a mellow, sober hue to the building. Another advantage of the climate is that it permits outside plastering. Thus almost any stone may be imitated, and the work endure for ages; while our sudden changes, and extremes of heat and cold, of dampness and dryness, will cause the best work of this kind to peel off in a few years.

Then this people have better taste in building than we have, perhaps because they have the noblest samples and specimens of architecture constantly before them,— those old feudal castles and royal residences, for instance. I was astonished to see how homely and good they looked, how little they challenged admiration, and how much they emulated rocks and trees. They were surely built in a simpler and more poetic age than this. It was like meeting some plain, natural nobleman after contact with one of the bedizened, artificial sort. The Tower of London, for instance, is as pleasing to the eye, has the same fitness and harmony, as a hut in the woods; and I should think an artist might have the same pleasure in copying it into his picture as he would in copying a pioneer's log cabin. So with Windsor Castle, which has the beauty of a ledge of rocks, and crowns the hill like a vast natural formation. The warm, simple interior, too, of these castles and palaces, the honest oak without paint or varnish, the rich wood carvings, the ripe human tone and atmosphere, — how it all contrasts, for instance, with the showy, gilded, cast-iron interior

of our commercial or political palaces, where everything that smacks of life or nature is studiously excluded under the necessity of making the building fire-proof.

I was not less pleased with the higher ornamental architecture, — the old churches and cathedrals, — which appealed to me in a way architecture had never before done. In fact, I found that I had never seen architecture before,— a building with genius and power in it, and that one could look at with the eye of the imagination. Not mechanics merely, but poets, had wrought and planned here, and the granite was tender with human qualities. The plants and weeds growing in the niches and hollows of the walls, the rooks and martins and jackdaws inhabiting the towers and breeding about the eaves, are but types of the feelings and emotions of the human heart that flit and hover over these old piles, and find affectionate lodgment in them.

Time, of course, has done a great deal for this old architecture. Nature has taken it lovingly to herself, has set her seal upon it, and adopted it into her system. Just the foil which beauty — especially the crystallic beauty of architecture — needs has been given by this hazy, mellowing atmosphere. As the grace and suggestiveness of all objects are enhanced by a fall of snow, — forest, fence, hive, shed, knoll, rock, tree, all being laid under the same white enchantment, — so time has wrought in softening and toning down this old religious architecture, and bringing it into harmony with nature.

Our climate has a much keener edge, both of frost and fire, and touches nothing so gently or creatively; yet time would, no doubt, do much for our architecture, if we would give it a chance, — for that apotheosis of prose, the National Capitol at Washington, upon which, I notice, a returned traveler bases our claim to be considered "ahead" of the Old World, even in architecture; but the reigning gods interfere, and each spring or fall give the building a clean shirt in the shape of a coat of white paint. In like manner, other public buildings never become acclimated, but are annually scoured with soap and sand, the national passion for the brightness of newness interfering to defeat any benison which the gods might be disposed to pronounce upon them. Spotlessness, I know, is not a characteristic of our politics, though it is said that whitewashing is, which may account for this ceaseless paint-pot renovation of our public buildings. In a world lit only by the moon, our Capitol would be a paragon of beauty, and the spring whitewashing could also be endured; but under our blazing sun and merciless sky it parches the vision, and makes it turn with a feeling of relief to rocks and trees, or to some weather-stained, dilapidated shed or hovel.

How winningly and picturesquely in comparison, the old architecture of London addresses itself to the eye,— St. Paul's Cathedral, for instance, with its vast blotches and stains, as if it had been dipped in some black Lethe of oblivion, and then left to be restored by the rains and the elements! This black

Lethe is the London smoke and fog, which has left a dark deposit over all the building, except the upper and more exposed parts, where the original silvery whiteness of the stone shows through, the eifect of the whole thus being like one of those graphic Kembrandt photographs or carbons, the prominences in a strong light, and the rest in deepest shadow. I was never tired of looking at this noble building, and of going out of my way to walk around it; but I am at a loss to know whether the pleasure I had in it arose from my love of nature, or from a susceptibility to art for which I had never given myself credit. Perhaps from both, for I seemed to behold Art turning toward and reverently acknowledging Nature,— indeed, in a manner already become Nature. I believe the critics of such things find plenty of fault with St. Paul's; and even I could see that its bigness was a little prosy, that it suggested the historic rather than the poetic muse, etc. ; yet, for all that, I could never look at it Avithout a profound emotion. Viewed coolly and critically, it might seem like a vast specimen of Episcopalianism in architecture. Miltonic in its grandeur and proportions, and Miltonic in its prosiness and mongrel classicism also, yet its power and effectiveness are unmistakable. The beholder has no vantage-ground from which to view it, or take in its total effect, on account of its being so closely beset by such a mob of shops and buildings; yet the glimpses he does get here and there through the opening made by some street, when passing in its vicinity, are very striking and

suggestive; the thin veil of smoke, which is here as constant and uniform as the atmbsphere itself, wrapping it about with the enchantment of time and distance.

The interior I found even more impressive than the exterior, perhaps because I was unprepared for it. I had become used to imposing exteriors at home, and did not reflect that in a structure like this I should see an interior also, and that here alone the soul of the building would be fully revealed. It was Miltonic in the best sense; it was like the mightiest organ music put into form. Such depths, such solemn vastness, such gulfs and abysses of architectural space, the rich, mellow light, the haze outside becoming a mysterious, hallowing presence within, quite mastered me, and I sat down upon a seat, feeling my first genuine cathedral intoxication. As it was really an intoxication, a sense of majesty and power quite overwhelming in my then uncloyed condition, I speak of it the more freely. My companions rushed about as if each one had had a search-warrant in his pocket; but I was content to uncover my head and drop into a seat, and busy my mind with some simple object near at hand, while the sublimity that soared about me stole into my soul and possessed it. My sensation was like that imparted by suddenly reaching a great altitude: there was a sort of relaxation of the muscles, followed by a sense of physical weakness; and after half an hour or so I felt compelled to go out into the open air, and leave till another day the final survey of the

building. Next day I came back, but there can be only one first time, and I could not again surprise myself with the same feeling of wonder and intoxication. But St. Paul's will bear many visits. I came again and again, and never grew tired of it. Crossing its threshold was entering another world, where the silence and solitude were so profound and overpowering that the noise of the streets outside, or of tlie stream of visitors, or of the workmen engaged on the statuary, made no impression. They were all belittled, lost, like the humming of flies. Even the afternoon services, the chanting, and the tremendous organ, were no interruption, and left me just as much alone as ever. They only served to set off the silence, to fathom its depth.

The dome of St. Paul's is the original of our dome at Washington; but externally I think ours is the more graceful of the two, though the effect inside is tame and flat in comparison. This is owing partly to the lesser size and height, and partly to our hard, transparent atmosphere, which lends no charm or illusion, but mainly to the stupid, unimaginative plan of it. Our dome shuts down like an inverted iron pot; there is no vista, no outlook, no relation, and hence no proportion. You open a door and are in a circular pen, and can look in only one direction,— up. If the iron pot were slashed through here and there, or if it rested on a row of tall columns or piers, and was shown to be a legitimate part of the building, it would not appear the exhausted receiver it does now.

The dome of St. Paul's is the culmination of the whole interior of the building. Rising over the central area, it seems to gather up the power and majesty of the nave, the aisles, the transepts, the choir, and give them expression and expansion in its lofty firmament.

Then those colossal piers, forty feet broad some of them, and nearly one hundred feet high,— they easily eclipsed what I had recently seen in a mine, and which I at the time imagined shamed all the architecture of the world,—where the mountain was upheld over a vast space by massive piers left by the miners, with a ceiling unrolled over your head, and apparently descending upon you, that looked like a petrified thunder-cloud.

The view from the upper gallery, or top of the dome, looking down inside, is most impressive. The public are not admitted to this gallery, for fear, the keeper told me, it would become the scene of suicides; people unable to withstand the terrible fascination would leap into the yawning gulf. But, with the privilege usually accorded to Americans, I stepped down into the narrow circle, and, leaning over the balustrade, coolly looked the horrible temptation in the face.

On the whole, St. Paul's is so vast and imposing that one wonders what occasion or what ceremony can rise to the importance of not being utterly dwarfed within its walls. The annual gathering of the charity children, ten or twelve thousand in number, must make a ripple or two upon its soli-

tilde, or an exhibition like the thanksgiving of the Queen, when sixteen or eighteen thousand persons were assembled beneath its roof. But one cannot forget that it is, for the most part, a great toy,— a mammoth shell, whose bigness bears no proportion to the living (if, indeed, it is living), indwelling necessity. It is a tenement so large that the tenant looks cold and forlorn, and in danger of being lost within it.

No such objection can be made to Westminster Abbey, which is a mellow, picturesque old place, the interior arrangement and architecture of which affects one like some ancient, dilapidated forest. Even the sunlight streaming through the dim windows, and falling athwart the misty air, was like the sunlight of a long-gone age. The very atmosphere was pensive, and .filled the tall spaces like a memory and a dream. I sat down and listened to the choral service and to the organ, which blended perfectly with the spirit and sentiment of the place.

ON THE SOUTH DOWNS

One of my best days in England was spent amid the singing of skylarks on the South Down Hills, near an old town at the mouth of the Little Ouse, where I paused on my way to France. The prospect of hearing one or two of the classical birds of the Old World had not been the least of the attractions of my visit, though I knew the chances were against me so late in the season, and I have to thank my good genius for guiding me to the right place at the right time. To get oTit of London was delight enough, and then to find myself quite unexpectedly on these soft rolling hills, of a mild October day, in full sight of the sea, with the larks pouring out their gladness overhead, was to me good fortune indeed.

The South Downs form a very remarkable feature of this part of England, and are totally unlike any other landscape I ever saw. I believe it is Huxley who applies to them the epithet of muttony^ which they certainly deserve, for they are like the backs of immense sheep, smooth, and round, and fat, — so smooth, indeed, that the eye can hardly find a place to take hold of, not a tree, or bush, or fence, or house, or rock, or stone, or other object, for miles and miles, save here and there a group of straw-capped stacks, or a flock of. sheep crawling slowly over them, attended by a shepherd and dog, and the only lines visible those which bound the squares where different crops had been gathered. The soil was rich and mellow, like a garden, — hills of chalk with a pellicle of black loam.

These hills stretch a great distance along the coast, and are cut squarely off by the sea, presenting on this side a chain of white chalk cliffs suggesting the old Latin name of this land, Albion.

Before I had got fifty yards from the station I began to hear the larks, and being unprepared for them I was a little puzzled at first, but was not long in discovering what luck I was in. The song disappointed me at first, being less sweet and melodious

than I had expected to hear; indeed, I thought it a little sharp and harsh, — a little stubbly, — but in other respects, in strength and gladness and continuity, it was wonderful. And the more I heard it the better I liked it, until I would gladly have given any of my songsters at home for a bird that could shower down such notes, even in autumn. Up, up, went the bird, describing a large easy spiral till he attained an altitude of three or four hundred feet, when, spread out against the sky for a space of ten or fifteen minutes or more, he poured out his delight, filling all the vault with sound. The song is of the sparrow kind, and, in its best parts, perpetually suggested the notes of our vesper sparrow; but the wonder of it is its copiousness and sustained strength. There is no theme, no beginning, middle, or end, like most of our best bird-songs, but a perfect swarm of notes pouring out like bees from a hive, and resembling each other nearly as closely, and only ceasing as the bird nears the earth again. We have many more melodious songsters ; the bobolink in the meadows for instance, the vesper sparrow in the pastures, the purple finch in the groves, the winter wren, or any of the thrushes in the woods, or the wood-wagtail, whose air song is of a similar character to that of the skylark's, and is even more rapid and ringing, and is delivered in nearly the same manner; but our birds all stop when the skylark has only just begun. Away he goes on quivering wing, inflating his throat fuller and fuller, mounting and mounting, and turning to

all points of the compass as if to embrace the whole landscape in his song, the notes still raining upon you, as distinct as ever, after you have left him far behind. You feel that you need be in no hurry to observe the song lest the bird finish; you walk along, your mind reverts to other things, you examine the grass and weeds, or search for a curious stone, still there goes the bird; you sit down and study the landscape, or send your thoughts out toward France or Spain, or across the sea to your own land, and yet, when you get them back, there is that song above you, almost as unceasing as the light of a star. This strain indeed suggests some rare pyrotechnic display, musical sounds being substituted for the many-colored sparks and lights. And yet I will add, what perhaps the best readers do not need to be told, that neither the lark-song, nor any other bird-song in the open air and under the sky, is as noticeable a feature as my description of it might imply, or as the poets would have us believe; and that most persons, not especially interested in birds or their notes, and intent upon the general beauty of the landscape, would probably pass it by unremarked.

I suspect that it is a little higher flight than the facts will bear out when the writers make the birds go out of sight into the sky. I could easily follow them on this occasion, though, if I took my eye away for a moment, it was very difficult to get it back again. I had to search for them as the astronomer searches for a star. It may be that in the

spring, when the atmosphere is less clear and the heart of the bird full of a more mad and reckless love, that the climax is not reached until the eye loses sight of the singer.

Several attempts have been made to introduce the lark into this country, but for some reason or other the experiment has never succeeded. The birds have been liberated in Virginia and on Long Island, but do not seem to have ever been heard of afterwards. I see no reason why they should not thrive anywhere along our Atlantic seaboard, and I think the question of introducing them worthy of more thorough and serious attention than has yet been given it, for the lark is really an institution; and as he sings long after the other birds are silent, — as if he had perpetual spring in his heart, — he would be a great acquisition to our fields and meadows. It may be that he cannot stand the extremes of our climate, though the English sparrow thrives well enough. The Smithsonian Institution has received specimens of the skylark from Alaska, where, no doubt, they find a climate more like the English.

They have another prominent singer in England, namely, the robin, — the original robin redbreast,— a slight, quick, active bird with an orange front and an olive back, and a bright, musical warble that I caught by every garden, lane, and hedge-row. It suggests our bluebird, and has similar habits and manners, though it is a much better musician.

The European bird that corresponds to our robin is the blackbird, of which Tennyson sings: —

"O Blackbird, sing me something well ; While all the neighbors shoot thee round I keep smooth plats of fruitful ground Where thou ma^^'st warble, eat, and dwell."

It quite startled me to see such a resemblance,— to see, indeed, a black robin. In size, form, flight, manners, note, call, there is hardly an appreciable difference. The bird starts up with the same flirt of the wings, and calls out in the same jocund, salutatory way, as he hastens off". The nest, of coarse mortar in the fork of a tree, or in an outbuilding, or in the side of a wall, is also the same.

The bird I wished most to hear, namely, the nightingale, had already departed on its southern journey. I saw one in the Zoological Gardens in London, and took a good look at him. He struck me as bearing a close resemblance to our hermit thrush, with something in his manners that suggested the water-thrush also. Carlyle said he first recognized its song from the description of it in "Wilhelm Meister," and that it was a "sudden burst," which is like the song of our water-thrush.

I have little doubt our songsters excel in melody, while the European birds excel in profuseness and volubility. I heard many bright, animated notes and many harsh ones, but few that were melodious. This fact did not harmonize with the general drift of the rest of my observations, for one of the first things that strikes an American in Europe is the mellowness and rich tone of things. The European is softer-voiced than the American and milder-mannered, but the bird voices seem an exception to this rule.

While in London I had much pleasure in strolling through the great parks, Hyde Park, Eegent's Park, St. James Park, Victoria Park, etc., and in making Sunday excursions to Eichmond Park or Hampden Court Parks, or the great parks at Windsor Castle. The magnitude of all these parks was something I was entirely unprepared for, and their freedom also; one could roam where he pleased. Not once did I see a signboard, "Keep off the grass," or go here or go there. There was grass enough, and one could launch out in every direction without fear of trespassing on forbidden ground. One gets used, at least I do, to such petty parks at home, and walks amid them so cautiously and circumspectly, every shrub and tree and grass plat saying "Hands off," that it is a new sensation to enter a city pleasure ground like Hyde Park, — a vast natural landscape, nearly two miles long and a mile wide, with broad, rolling plains, with herds of sheep grazing, and forests and lakes, and all as free as the air. We have some quite sizable parks and reservations in Washington, and the citizen has the right of way over their tortuous gravel walks, but he puts his foot upon the grass at the risk of being insolently hailed by the local police. I have even been called to order for reclining upon a seat under a tree in the Smithsonian grounds. I must sit upright as in church. But in Hyde Park or Regent's Park I could not only walk upon the grass, but lie upon

it, or roll upon it, or play " one catch all" with children, boys, dogs, or sheep upon it; and I took my revenge for once for being so long confined to gravel walks, and gave the grass an opportunity to grow under my foot whenever I entered one of these parks.

This free-and-easy rural character of the London parks is quite in keeping with the tone and atmosphere of the great metropolis itself, which in so many respects has a country homeliness and sincerity, and shows the essentially bucolic taste of the people; contrasting in this respect with the parks and gardens of Paris, which show as unmistakably the citizen and the taste for art and the beauty of design and ornamentation. Hyde Park seems to me the perfection of a city pleasure ground of this kind, because it is so free and so thoroughly a piece of the country, and so exempt from any petty artistic displays.

In walking over Richmond Park I found I had quite a day's work before me, as it was like traversing a township; while the great park at Windsor Castle, being upwards of fifty miles around, might well make the boldest pedestrian hesitate. My first excursion was to Hampden Court, an old royal residence, where I spent a delicious October day wandering through Bushy Park, and looking with covetous, though admiring eyes upon the vast herds of deer that dotted the plains, or gave way before me as I entered the woods. There seemed literally to be many thousands of these beautiful animals in thia

park, and the loud, hankering sounds of the bucks, as they pursued or circled around the does, was a new sound to my ears. The rabbits and pheasants also were objects of the liveliest interest to me, and I found that after all a good shot at them with the eye, especially when I could credit myself with alertness or stealthiness, was satisfaction enough. ^ I thought it worthy of note that, though these great parks in and about London were so free, and apparently without any police regulations whatever, yet I never saw prowling about them any of those vicious, ruffianly-looking characters that generally infest the neighborhood of our great cities, especially of a Sunday. There were troops of boys, but they were astonishingly quiet and innoxious, very unlike American boys, white or black, a band of whom making excursions into the country are always a band of outlaws. Euffianism with us is no doubt much more brazen and pronounced, not merely because the law is lax, but because such is the genius of the people.

ENGLISH CHARACTERISTICS

England is a mellow country, and the English people are a mellow people. They have hung on the tree of nations a long time, and will, no doubt, hang as much longer; for windfalls, I reckon, are not the order in this island. We are pitched several degrees higher in this country. By contrast, things here are loud, sharp, and garish. Our geography is loud; the manners of the people are loud; our climate is loud, very loud, so dry and sharp, and full of violent changes and contrasts; and our goings-out and comings-in as a nation are anything but silent. Do we not occasionally give the door an extra slam just for effect ?

In England everything is on a lower key, slower, steadier, gentler. Life is, no doubt, as full, or fuller, in its material forms and measures, but less violent and aggressive. The buffers the English have between their cars to break the shock are typical of much one sees there.

All sounds are softer in England; the surface of things is less hard. The eye of day and the face of Nature are less bright. Everything has a mellow, subdued cast. There is no abruptness in the land-
scape, no sharp and violent contrasts, no brilliant and striking tints in the foliage. A soft, pale yellow is all one sees in the way of tints along the borders of the autumn woods. English apples (very small and inferior, by the way) are not so highly colored as ours. The blackberries, just ripening in October, are less pungent and acid; and the garden vegetables, such as cabbage, celery, cauliflower, beet, and other root crops, are less rank and fibrous; and I am very sure that the meats also are tenderer and sweeter. There can be no doubt about the superiority of mutton; and the tender and succulent grass, and the moist and agreeable climate, must tell upon the beef also.

English coal is all soft coal, and the stone is soft stone. The foundations of the hills are chalk instead of granite. The stone with which most of the old churches and cathedrals are built would not endure in our climate half a century; but in Britain the tooth of Time is much blunter, and the hunger of the old man less ravenous, and the ancient architecture stands half a millennium, or until it is slowly worn away by the gentle attrition of the wind and rain.

At Chester, the old Roman wall that surrounds the town, built in the first century and repaired in the ninth, is still standing without a break or a swerve, though in some places the outer face of the wall is worn through. The Cathedral, and St. John's Church, in the same town, present to the beholder outlines as jagged and broken as rocks and cliffs;
and yet it is only chip by chip, or grain by grain, that ruin approaches. The timber also lasts an incredibly long time. Beneath one of the arched ways, in the Chester wall above referred to, I saw timbers that must have been in place five or six hundred years. The beams in the old houses, also fully exposed to the weather, seem incapable of decay; those dating from Shakespeare's time being apparently as firm as ever.

I noticed that the characteristic aspect of the clouds in England was different from ours, — soft, fleecy, vapory, indistinguishable, — never the firm, compact, sharply-defined, deeply-dyed masses and fragments so common in our own sky. It rains easily but slowly. The average rainfall of London is less than that of New York, and yet it doubtless rains ten days in the former to one in the latter. Storms accompanied with thunder are rare; while the crashing, wrenching, explosive thunder-gusts so common with us, deluging the earth and convulsing the heavens, are seldom known.

In keeping with this elemental control and moderation, I found the character and manners of the people gentler and sweeter than I had been led to believe they were. No loudness, brazenness, impertinence; no oaths, no swaggering, no leering at women, no irreverence, no flippancy, no bullying, no insolence of porters or clerks or conductors, no importunity of bootblacks or newsboys, no omniv-orousness of hackmen, — at least, comparatively none, — all of which an American is apt to notice,
and I hope appreciate. In London the bootblack sakites you with a respectful bow and touches his cap, and would no more think of pursuing you or answering your refusal than he

would of jumping into the Thames. The same is true of the newsboys. If they were to scream and bellow in London as they do in New York or Washington, they would be suppressed by the police, as they ought to be. The vender of papers stands at the corner of the street, with his goods in his arms, and a large placard spread out at his feet, giving in big letters the principal news-headings.

Street-cries of all kinds are less noticeable, less aggressive, than in this country, and the manners of the shopmen make you feel you are conferring a benefit instead of receiving one. Even their locomotives are less noisy than ours, having a shrill, infantile whistle that contrasts strongly with the loud, demoniac yell that makes a residence near a railway or depot, in this country, so unbearable. The trains themselves move with wonderful smoothness and celerity, making a mere fraction of the racket made by our flying palaces as they go swaying and jolting over our hasty, ill-ballasted roads.

It is characteristic of the English prudence and plain dealing, that they put so little on the cars and so much on the road, while the reverse process is equally characteristic of American enterprise. Our railway system no doubt has certain advantages, or rather conveniences, over the English, but, for my part, I had rather ride smoothly, swiftly, and safely

in a luggage van than be jerked and jolted to destruction in the velvet and veneering of our palace cars. Upholster the road first, and let us ride on bare boards until a cushion can be afforded; not till after the bridges are of granite and iron, and the rails of steel, do we want this more than aristocratic splendor and luxury of palace and drawing-room cars. To me there is no more marked sign of the essential vulgarity of the national manners than these princely cars and beggarly, clap-trap roads. It is like a man wearing a ruffled and jeweled shirt-front, but too poor to afford a shirt itself.

I have said the English are a sweet and mellow people. There is, indeed, a charm about these ancestral races that goes to the heart. And herein was one of the profoundest surprises of my visit, namely, that, in coming from the New World to the Old, from a people the most recently out of the woods of any, to one of the ripest and venerablest of the European nationalities, I should find a race more simple, youthful, and less sophisticated than the one I had left behind me. Yet this was my impression. We have lost immensely in some things, and what we have gained is not yet so obvious or so definable. We have lost in reverence, in homeliness, in heart and conscience, — in virtue, using the word in its proper sense. To some, the difference which I note may appear a difference in favor of the greater 'cuteness, wideaAvakeness, and enterprise of the American, but is simply a difference expressive of our greater forwardness. We are

a forward people, and the god we worship is Smartness. In one of the worst tendencies of the age, namely, an impudent, superficial, journalistic intellectuality and glibness, America, in her polite and literary circles, no doubt leads all other nations. English books and newspapers show more homely veracity, more singleness of purpose, in short more character^ than ours. The great charm of such a man as Darwin, for instance, is his simple manliness and transparent good faith, and the absence in him of that finical, self-complacent smartness which is the bane of our literature.

The poet Clough thought the New England man more simple than the man of Old England. Hawthorne, on the other hand, seemed reluctant to admit that the English were a "franker and simpler people, from peer to peasant," than we are; and that they had not yet wandered so far from that " healthful and primitive simplicity in which man was created " as have their descendants in America. My own impression accords with Hawthorne's. We are a more alert and curious people, but not so simple, — not so easily angered, nor so easily amused. We have partaken more largely of the fruit of the forbidden tree. The English have more of the stay-at-home virtues, which, on the other hand, they no doubt pay pretty well for by their more insular tendencies.

The youths and maidens seemed more simple, with their softer and less intellectual faces. When I returned from Paris, the only person in the second-class

compartments of the car with me, for a long distance, was an English youth eighteen or twenty years old, returning home to London after an absence of nearly a year, which he had spent as waiter in a Parisian hotel. He was born in London and had spent nearly his whole life there, where his mother, a widow, then lived. He talked very freely with me, and told me his troubles, and plans, and hopes, as if we had long known each other. What especially struck me in the youth was a kind of sweetness and innocence — perhaps what some would call " greenness " — that at home I had associated only with country boys, and not even yvith them latterly. The smartness and knowingness and a certain hardness or keenness of our city youths, — there was no trace of it at all in this young Cockney. But he liked American travelers better than those from his own country. They were more friendly and communicative, — were not so afraid to speak to "a fellow," and at the hotel were more easily pleased.

The American is certainly not the grumbler the Englishman is; he is more cosmopolitan and conciliatory. The Englishman will not adapt himself to his surroundings; he is not the least bit an imitative animal; he will be nothing but an Englishman, and is out of place — an anomaly — in any country but his own. To understand him, you must see him at home in the British island where he grew, where he belongs, where he has expressed himself and justified himself, and his interior, unconscious characteristics are revealed. There he is quite a difierent

creature from what he is abroad. There he is " sweet," but he sours the moment he steps ofif the island. In this country he is too generally arrogant, fault-finding, and supercilious. The very traits of loudness, sharpness, and unleavenedness, which I complain of in our national manners, he very frequently exemplifies in an exaggerated form.

The Scotch or German element no doubt fuses and mixes with ours much more readily than the purely British.

The traveler feels the past in England as of course he cannot feel it here; and, along with impressions of the present, one gets the flavor and influence of earlier, simpler times, which, no doubt, is a potent charm, and one source of the "rose-color" which some readers have found in my sketches, as the absence of it is one cause of the raw, acrid, unlovely character of much there is in this country. If the English are the old wine, we are the new. We are not yet thoroughly leavened as a people, nor have we more than begun to transmute and humanize our surroundings; and, as the digestive and assimilative powers of the American are clearly less than those of the Englishman, to say nothing of our harsher, more violent climate, I have no idea that ours can ever become the mellow land that Britain is.

As for the charge of brutality that is often brought against the English, and which is so successfully depicted by Dickens and Thackeray, there is doubtless good ground for it, though I actually saw very

little of it during five weeks' residence in London, and I poked about into all the dens and corners I could find, and perambulated the streets at nearly all hours of the night and day. Yet I am persuaded there is a kind of brutality among the lower orders in England that does not exist in the same measure in this country,—an ignorant animal coarseness, an insensibility, which gives rise to wife-beating and kindred offenses. But the brutality of ignorance and stolidity is not the worst form of the evil. It is good material to make something better of. It is an excess and not a perversion. It is not man fallen, but man undeveloped. Beware, rather, that refined, subsidized brutality; that thin, depleted, moral consciousness; or that contemptuous, cankerous, euphemistic brutality, of which, I believe, we can show vastly more samples than Great Britain. Indeed, I believe, for the most part, that the brutality of the English people is only the excess and plethora of that healthful, muscular robustness and full-blood-edness for which the nation has always been famous, and which it should prize beyond almost anything else. But for our brutality, our recklessness of life and property, the brazen ruffianism in our great cities, the hellish greed and robbery and plunder in high places, I should have to look a long time to find so plausible an excuse.

[But I notice with pleasure that English travelers are beginning to find more to admire than to condemn in this country, and that they accredit us with some virtues they do not find at home in the

same measure. They are charmed with the independence, the self-r^pect, the good-nature, and the obliging dispositions shown by the mass of our people; while American travelers seem to be more and more ready to acknowledge the charm and the substantial qualities of the mother country. It is a good omen. One principal source of the pleasure which each takes in the other is no doubt to be found in the novelty of the impressions. It is like a change of cookery. The flavor of the dish is fresh and uncloying to each. The English probably tire of their own snobbishness and flunkeyism, and we of our own smartness and puppyism. After the Am.erican has got done bragging about his independence, and his "free and equal" prerogatives, he begins to see how these things run into impertinence and forwardness; and the Englishman, in visiting us, escapes from his social bonds and prejudices, to see for a moment how absurd they all are.]

A London crowd I thought the most normal and unsophisticated I had ever seen, with the least admixture of rowdyism and ruffianism. No doubt it is there, but this scum is not upon the surface, as with us. I went about very freely in the hundred and one places of amusement where the average working classes assemble, with their wives and daughters and sweethearts, and smoke villainous cigars and drink ale and stout. There was to me something notably fresh and canny about them, as if they had only yesterday ceased to be shepherds and shepherdesses. They certainly were less developed in

certain directions, or shall I say depraved, than similar crowds in our great cities. They are easily pleased, and laugh at the simple and childlike, but there is little that hints of an impure taste, or of abnormal appetites. I often smiled at the tameness and simplicity of the amusements, but my sense of fitness, or proportion, or decency was never once outraged. They always stop short of a certain point, — the point where wit degenerates into mockery, and liberty into license: nature is never put to shame, and will commonly bear much more. Especially to the American sense did their humorous and comic strokes, their negro-minstrelsy and attempts at Yankee comedy, seem in a minor key. There was not enough irreverence and slang and coarse ribaldry, in the whole evening's entertainment, to have seasoned one line of some of our most popular comic poetry. But the music, and the gymnastic, acrobatic, and other feats, were of a very high order. And I will say here that the characteristic flavor of the humor and fun-making of the average English people, as it impressed my sense, is what one gets in Sterne,— very human and stomachic, and entirely free from the contempt and superciliousness of most current writers. I did not get one whiff of Dickens anywhere. No doubt it is there in some form or other, but it is not patent, or even appreciable, to the sense of such an observer as I am.

I was not less pleased by the simple good-will and bonhomie that pervaded the crowd.

There is in all these gatherings an indiscriminate mingling of
the sexes, a mingling without jar or noise or rudeness of any kind, and marked by a mutual respect on all sides that is novel and refreshing. Indeed, so uniform is the courtesy, and so human and considerate the interest, that I was often at a loss to discriminate the wife or the sister from the mistress or the acquaintance of the hour, and had many times to check my American curiosity and cold, criticising stare. For it was curious to see young men and women from the lowest social strata meet and mingle in a public hall without lewdness or badinage, but even with gentleness and consideration. The truth is, however, that the class of women known as victims of the social evil do not sink within many degrees as low in Europe as they do in this country, either in their own opinion or in that of the public; and there can be but little doubt that gatherings of the kind referred to, if permitted in our great cities, would be tenfold more scandalous and disgraceful than they are in London or Paris. There is something so reckless and desperate in the career of man or woman in this country, when they begin to go down, that the only feeling they too often excite is one of loathsomeness and disgust. The lowest depth must be reached, and it is reached quickly. But in London the same characters seem to keep a sweet side from corruption to the last, and you will see good manners everywhere.

We boast of our deference to woman, but, if the Old World made her a tool, we are fast making hei
a toy; and the latter is the more hopeless condition. But among the better classes in England I am convinced that woman is regarded more as a sister and an equal than in this country, and is less subject to insult, and to leering, brutal comment, there than here. We are her slave or her tyrant; so seldom her brother and friend. I thought it a significant fact that I found no place of amusement set apart for the men; where one sex went the other went; what was sauce for the gander was sauce for the goose; and the spirit that prevailed was soft and human accordingly. The hotels had no "ladies' entrance," but all passed in and out the same door, and met and mingled commonly in the same room, and the place was as much for one as for the other. It was no more a masculine monopoly than it was a feminine. Indeed, in the country towns and villages the character of the inns is unmistakably given by woman; hence the sweet, domestic atmosphere that pervades and fills them is balm to the spirit. Even the larger hotels of Liverpool and London have a private, cosy, home character that is most delightful. On entering them, instead of finding yourself in a sort of public thoroughfare or political caucus, amid crowds of men talking and smoking and spitting, with stalls on either side where cigars and tobacco and books and papers are sold, you perceive you are in something like a larger hall of a private house, with perhaps a parlor and coffee-room on one side, and the office, and smoking-room, and stairway on the other. You may leave your coat and
hat on the rack in the hall, and stand your umbrella there also, with full assurance that you will find them there when you want them, if it be the next morning or the next week. Instead of that petty tyrant the hotel clerk, a young woman sits in the office with her sewing or other needlework, and quietly receives you. She gives you your number on a card, rings for a chambermaid to show you to your room, and directs your luggage to be sent up; and there is something in the look of things, and the way they are done, that goes to the right spot at once.

At the hotel in London where I stopped, the daughters of the landlord, three fresh, comely young women, did the duties of the office; and their presence, so quiet and domestic, gave the prevailing hue and tone to the whole house. I wonder how long a young woman could preserve her self-respect and sensibility in such a position in New York or Washington ?

The English regard us as a wonderfully patient people, and there can be no doubt but we put up with abuses unknown elsewhere. If we have no big tyrant, we have ten thousand little ones, who tread upon our toes at every turn. The tyranny of corporations, and of public servants of one kind and another, as the ticket-man, the railroad conductor, or even of the country stage-driver, seem to be features peculiar to American democracy. In England the traveler is never snubbed, or made to feel that it is by somebody's sufferance that he is allowed aboard or to pass on his way.

If you get into an omnibus or a railroad or tramway carriage in London, you are sure of a seat. Not another person can get aboard after the seats are all full. Or, if you enter a public hall, you know you will not be required to stand up unless you pay the standing-up price. There is everywhere that system, and order, and fair dealing, which all men love. The science of living has been reduced to a fine point. You pay a sixpence and get a sixpence worth of whatever you buy. There are all grades and prices, and the robbery and extortion so current at home appear to be unknown.

I am not contending for the superiority of everything English, but would not disguise from myself or my readers the fact of the greater humanity and consideration that prevail in the mother country. Things here are yet in the green, but I trust there is no good reason to doubt that our fruit will mellow and ripen in time like the rest.

HI

A GLIMPSE OF FRANCE

In coming over to France, I noticed that the chalk-hills, which were stopped so abruptly by the sea on the British side of the Channel, began again on the French side, only they had lost their smooth, pastoral character, and were more broken and rocky, and that they continued all the way to Paris, walling in the Seine, and giving the prevailing tone and hue to the country, — scrape away the green and brown epidermis of the hills anywhere, and out shine their white framework, — and that Paris itself was built of stone evidently quarried from this formation, — a light, cream-colored stone, so soft that rifle-bullets bury themselves in it nearly their own depth, thus pitting some of the more exposed fronts during the recent strife in a very noticeable manner, and which, in building, is put up in the rough, all the carving, sculpturing, and finishing being done after the blocks are in position in the wall.

Disregarding the counsel of friends, I braved the Channel at one of its wider points, taking the vixen by the waist instead of by the neck, and found her as placid as a lake, as I did also on my return a week later.

It was a bright October morning as we steamed into the little liarboy at Dieppe, and the first scene that met my eye was, I suppose, a characteristic one, — four or five old men and women towing a vessel into a dock. They bent beneath the rope that passed from shoulder to shoulder, and tugged away doggedly at it, the women apparently more than able to do their part. There is no equalizer of the sexes like poverty and misery, and then it very often happens that the gray mare proves the better horse. Throughout the agricultural regions, as we passed along, the men apparently all wore petticoats; at least, the petticoats were the most active and prominent in the field occupations. Their wearers were digging potatoes, pulling beets, following the harrow (in one instance a thorn-bush drawn by a cow), and stirring the wet, new-mown grass. I believe the pantaloons were doing the mowing. But I looked in vain for any Maud Mullers in the meadows, and have concluded that these can only be found in New England hay-fields! And herein is one of the first surprises that aAvaits one on visiting the Old World countries,— the absence of graceful, girlish figures, and bright girlish faces, among the peasantry or rural population. In France I certainly expected to see female beauty everywhere, but did not get one gleam all that sunny day till I got to Paris. Is it a plant that only flourishes in cities on this side of the Atlantic, or do all the pretty girls, as soon as they are grown, pack their trunks, and leave for the gay metropolis ?

At Dieppe I first saw the wooden shoe, and heard its dry, senseless clatter upon the pavement. How suggestive of the cramped and inflexible conditions with which human nature has borne so long in these lands!

A small paved square near the wharf was the scene of an early market, and afl'orded my first glimpse of the neatness and good taste that characterize nearly everything in France. Twenty or thirty peasant women, coarse and masculine, but very tidy, with their snow-white caps and short petticoats, and perhaps half as many men, were chattering and chaffering over little heaps of fresh country produce. The onions and potatoes and cauliflowers, etc., were prettily arranged on the clean pavement, or on white linen cloths, and the scene was altogether animated and agreeable.

La belle France is the woman's countiy clearly, and it seems a mistake or an anomaly that woman is not at the top and leading in all departments, compelling the other sex to play second fiddle, as she so frequently has done for a brief time in isolated cases in the past; not that the man is effeminate, but that the woman seems so nearly his match and equal, and even so often proves his superior. In no other nation, during times of popular excitement and insurrection or revolution, do women emerge so conspicuously, often in the front ranks, the most furious and ungovernable of any. I think even a female conscription might be advisable in the present condition of France, if I may judge of her

soldiers from the specimens I saw. Small, spiritless, inferior-looking men all of them. They were like Number Three mackerel or the last run of shad, as doubtless they were, — the last pickings and re-siftings of the population.

I don't know how far it may be a national custom, but I observed that the women of the humbler classes, in meeting or parting with friends at the stations, saluted each other on both cheeks, never upon the mouth, as our dear creatures do, and I commended their good taste, though I certainly approve the American custom, too.

Among the male population I was struck with the frequent recurrence of the Louis Napoleon type of face. "Has this man," I said, "succeeded in impressing himself even upon the physiognomy of the people ? Has he taken such a hold of their imaginations that they have grown to look like him 1 " The guard that took our train down to Paris might easily play the double to the ex-emperor; and many times in Paris and among different classes I saw the same countenance.

Coming from England, the traveling seems very slow in this part of France, taking eight or nine hours to go from Dieppe to Paris, with an hour's delay at Kouen. The valley of the Seine, which the road follows or skirts more than half the way, is very winding, with immense flats or plains shut in by a wall of steep, uniform hills, and, in the progress of the journey, is from time to time laid open to the traveler in a way that is full of novelty

and surprise. The day was bright and lovely, and I found my eyes running riot the same as they had done during my first ride on British soil. The contrast between the two countries is quite marked, France in this region being much more broken and picturesque, with some waste or sterile land, — a thing I did not see at all in England. Had I awoke from a long sleep just before reaching Paris, I should have guessed I was riding through Maryland, and should soon see the dome of the Capitol at Washington rising above the trees. So much wild and bushy or barren and half-cultivated land, almost under the walls of the French capital, was a surprise.

Then there are few or none of those immense home-parks which one sees in England, the land being mostly held by a great number of small proprietors, and cultivated in strips, or long, narrow parallelograms, making the landscape look like many-colored patchwork. Everywhere along the Seine, stretching over the flats, or tilted up against the sides of the hills, in some places seeming almost to stand on end, were these acre or half-acre rectangular farms, without any dividing lines or fences, and of a great variety of shades and colors, according to the crop and the tillage.

I was glad to see my old friend, the beech-tree, all along the route. His bole wore the same gray and patched appearance it does at home, and no doubt Thoreau would have found his instep even fairer; for the beech on this side of the Atlantic is a

more fluent and graceful tree than the American species, resembling, in its branchings and general form, our elm, though never developing such an immense green dome as our elm when standing alone, and I saw no European tree that does. The European elm is not unlike our beech in form and outline.

Going from London to Paris is, in some respects, like getting out of the chimney on to the housetop, — the latter city is, by contrast, so light and airy, and so American in its roominess. I had come to Paris for my dessert after my feast of London joints, and I suspect I was a little dainty in that most dainty of cities. In fact, I had become quite sated with sight-seeing, and the prospect of having to go on and " do " the rest of Europe after the usual manner of tourists, and as my companions did, would have been quite appalling. Said companions steered off like a pack of foxhounds in full blast. The game they were in quest of led them a wild chase up the Rhine, off through Germany and Italy, taking a turn back through Switzerland, giving them no rest, and apparently eluding them at last. I had felt obliged to cut loose from them at the outset, my capacity to digest kingdoms and empires at short notice being far below that of the average of my countrymen. My interest and delight had been too intense at the outset; I had partaken too heartily of the first courses; and now, where other travelers begin to warm to the subject, and to have the keenest relish, I began to wish the whole thing well through with. So that Paris was no paradise to one Ameri-

can at least. Yet the mere change of air and sky, and the escape from that sooty, all-pervasive, chimney-flue smell of London, was so sudden and complete, that the first hour of Paris was like a refreshing bath, and gave rise to satisfaction in which every pore of the skin participated. My room at the hotel was a gem of neatness and order, and the bed a marvel of art, comfort, and ease, three feet deep at least.

Then the uniform imperial grace and eclat of the city was a new experience. Here was the city of cities, the capital of taste and fashion, the pride and flower of a great race and a great history, the city of kings and emperors, and of a people which, after all, loves kings and emperors, and will not long, I fear, be happy without them, — a gregarious, urbane people, a people of genius and destiny, whose God is Art and whose devil is Communism. London has long ago outgrown itself, has spread, and multiplied, and accumulated, without a corresponding inward expansion and unification; but in Paris they have pulled down and built larger, and the spirit of centralization has had full play. Hence the French capital is superb, but soon grows monotonous. See one street and boulevard, and you have seen it all. It has the unity and consecutiveness of a thing deliberately planned and built to order, from beginning to end. Its stone is all from one quarry, and its designs all the work of one architect. London has infinite variety, and quaintness, and picturesqueness, and is of all possible shades of din-

giness and weather-stains. It shows its age, shows the work of innumerable generations, and is more an aggregation, a conglomeration, than Paris is. Paris shows the citizen, and is modern and democratic in its uniformity. On the whole, I liked London best, because I am so much of a countryman, I suppose, and affect so little the metropolitan spirit. In London there are a few grand things to be seen, and the pulse of the great city itself is like the throb of the ocean; but in Paris, owing either to my jaded senses or some other cause, I saw nothing that was grand, but enough that was beautiful and pleasing. The more pretentious and elaborate specimens of architecture, like the Palace of the Tuileries or the Palais Royal, are truly superb, but they as truly do not touch that deeper chord whose awakening we call the emotion of the sublime. But the fitness and good taste everywhere displayed in the French capital may well offset any considerations of this kind, and cannot fail to be refreshing to a traveler of any other land, — in the dress and manners of the people, in the shops and bazaars and show-windows, in the markets, the equipages, the furniture, the hotels. It is entirely a new sensation to an American to look into a Parisian theatre, and see the acting and hear the music. The chances are that, for the first time, he sees the interior of a theatre that does not have a hard, business-like, matter-of-fact air. The auditors look comfortable and cosy, and quite at home, and do not, shoulder to shoulder and in solid lines, make a

dead set at the play and the music. The theatre has warm hangings, warm colors, cosy hoxes and stalls, and is in no sense the public, away-from-home place we are so familiar with in this country. Again, one might know it was Paris by the character of the prints and pictures in the shop windows; they are so clever as art, one becomes reprehensi-bly indifferent to their license. Whatever sins the French may be guilty of, they never sin against art and good taste (except when in the frenzy of revolution), and, if Propriety is sometimes obliged to cry out " For shame! " in the French capital, she must do so with ill-concealed admiration, like a fond mother chiding with word and gesture while she approves with tone and look. It is a foolish charge, often made, that the French make vice attractive: they make it provocative of laughter; the spark of wit is always evolved, and what is a better antidote to this kind of poison than mirth?

They carry their wit even into their cuisine. Every dish set before you at the table is a picture, and tickles your eye before it does your palate. When I ordered fried eggs, they were brought on a snow-white napkin, which was artistically folded upon a piece of ornamented tissue-paper that covered a china plate; if I asked for cold ham, it came in flakes, arrayed like great rose-leaves, with a green sprig or two of parsley dropped upon it, and surrounded by a border of calves-foot jelly, like a setting of crystals. The bread revealed new qualities in the wheat, it was so sweet and nutty; and

the fried potatoes, with which your beefsteak conies snowed under, are the very flower of the culinary art, and I believe impossible in any other country.

Even the ruins are in excellent taste, and are by far the best-behaved ruins I ever saw for so recent ones. I came near passing some of the most noted, during my first walk, without observing them. The main walls were all standing, and the fronts were as imposing as ever. No litter or rubbish, no charred timbers or blackened walls; only vacant windows and wrecked interiors, which do not very much mar the general outside effect.

My first genuine surprise was the morning after my arrival, which, according to my reckoning, was Sunday; and when I heard the usual week-day sounds, and, sallying forth, saw the usual week-day occupations going on, — painters painting, glaziers glazing, masons on their scaffolds, etc., and heavy drays and market-wagons going through the streets, and many shops and bazaars open, — I must have presented to a scrutinizing beholder the air and manner of a man in a dream, so absorbed was I in running over the events of the week to find where the mistake had occurred, where I had failed to turn a leaf, or else had turned over two leaves for one. But each day had a distinct record, and every count resulted the same. It must be Sunday. Then it all dawned upon me that this was Paris, and that the Parisians did not have the reputation of being very strict Sabbatarians.

The French give a touch of art to whatever they do. Even the drivers of drays and carts and trucks about the streets are not content with a plain, matter-of-fact whip, as an English or American laborer would be, but it must be a finely-modeled stalk, with a long, tapering lash tipped with the best silk snapper. Always the inevitable snapper. I doubt if there is a whip in Paris without a snapper. Here is where the fine art, the rhetoric of driving, comes in. This converts a vulgar, prosy "gad" into a delicate instrument, to be wielded with pride and skill, and never to be literally applied to the backs of the animals, but to be launched to the right and left into the air with a professional flourish, and a sharp, ringing report. Crack! crack! crack! all day long go these ten thousand whips, like the boys' Fourth of July fusillade. It was invariably the first sound I heard when I opened my eyes in the morning, and generally the last one at night. Occasionally some belated drayman would come hurrying along just as I was going to sleep, or some early bird before I was fully awake in the morning, and let off in rapid succession, in front of my hotel, a volley from the tip of his lash that would make the street echo again, and that might well have been the envy of any ring-master that ever trod the tan-bark. Now^and then, during my ramblings, I would suddenly hear some master-whip, perhaps that of an old omnibus-driver, that would crack like a rifle, and, as it passed along, all the lesser whips, all the amateur snappers, would strike up with a jealous and envious emulation, making every foot-passenger wink, and one (myself) at least almost to shade his eyes from the imaginary missiles.

I record this fact because it " points a moral and adorns a ' tail.' " The Erench always give this extra touch. Everything has its silk snapper. Are not the literary whips of Paris famous for their rhetorical tips and the sting there is in them? What French writer ever goaded his adversary with the belly of his lash, like the Germans and English, when he could blister him with its silken end, and the percussion of wit be heard at every stroke ?

In the shops, and windows, and public halls, etc., this passion takes the form of mirrors, —mirrors, mirrors everywhere, on the walls, in the panels, in the cases, on the pillars, extending, multiplying, opening up vistas this way and that, and converting the smallest shop, with a solitary girl and a solitary customer, into an immense enchanted bazaar, across whose endless counters customers lean and pretty girls display goods. The Erench are always before the looking-glass, even when they eat and drink. I never went into a restaurant without seeing four or five fac-similes of myself approaching from as many different directions, giving the order to the waiter and sitting down at the table. Hence I always had plenty of company at dinner, though we were none of us very social, and I was the only one who entered or passed out at the door. The show-windows are the greatest cheat. What an expanse, how crowded, and how brilliant! You see, for instance, an immense array of jewelry, and

pause to have a look. You begin at the end nearest you, and, after gazing a moment, take a step to run your eye along the dazzling display, when, presto! the trays of watches and diamonds vanish in a twinkling, and you find yourself looking into the door, or your delighted eyes suddenly bring up against a brick wall, disenchanted so quickly that you almost stagger.

I went into a popular music and dancing hall one night, and found myself in a perfect enchantment of mirrors. Not an inch of wall was anywhere visible. I was suddenly caught up into the seventh heaven of looking-glasses, from which I came down with a shock the moment I emerged into the street again. I observed that this mirror contagion had broken out in spots in London, and, in the narrow and crowded condition of the shops there, even this illusory enlargement would be a relief. It might not improve the air, or add to the available storage capacity of the establishment, but it would certainly give a wider range to the eye.

The American no sooner sets foot on the soil of France than he perceives he has entered a nation of drinkers as he has left a nation of eaters. Men do not live by bread here, but by wine. Drink, drink, drink everywhere, — along all the boulevards, and streets, and quays, and byways; in the restaurants and under awnings, and seated on the open sidewalk; social and convivial wine-bibbing, — not hastily and in large quantities, but leisurely and reposingly, and with much conversation and enjoyment.

Drink, drink, drink, and, with equal frequency and nearly as much openness, the reverse or diuretic side of the fact. (How our self-consciousness would writhe! We should all turn to stone!) Indeed, the ceaseless deglutition of mankind in this part of the world is only equaled by the answering and enormous activity of the human male kidneys. This latter was too astonishing and too public a fact to go unmentioned. At Dieppe, by the reeking tubs standing about, I suspected some local distemper; but when I got to Paris, and saw how fully and openly the wants of the male citizen in this respect were recognized by the sanitary and municipal regulations, and that the urinals were thicker than the lamp-posts, I concluded it must be a national trait, and at once abandoned the theory that had begun to take possession of my mind, namely, that diabetes was no doubt the cause of the decadence of France. Yet I suspect it is no more a peculiarity of French manners than of European manners generally, and in its light I relished immensely the history of a well-known statue which stands in a public square in one of the German cities. The statue commemorates the unblushing audacity of a peasant going to market with a goose under each arm, who ignored even the presence of the king, and it is at certain times dressed up and made the centre of holiday festivities. It is a public fountain, and its living streams of water make it one of the most appropriate and suggestive monuments in Europe. I would only suggest that they canonize the Little Man,

and that the Parisians recognize a tutelar deity in the goddess Urea, who should have an appropriate monument somewhere in the Place de la Concorde I

One of the loveliest features of Paris is the Seine. I was never tired of walking along its course. Its granite embankments; its numberless superb bridges, throwing their graceful spans across it; its clear, limpid water; its paved bed; the women washing; the lively little boats; and the many noble buildings that look down upon it, — make it the most charming citizen-river I ever beheld. Rivers generally get badly soiled when they come to the city, like some other rural travelers; but the Seine is as pure as a meadow-brook wherever I saw it, though I dare say it does not escape without some contamination. I believe it receives the sewerage discharges farther down, and is no doubt turbid and pitchy enough there, like its brother, the Thames, which comes into London with the sky and the clouds in its bosom, and leaves it reeking with filth and slime.

After I had tired of the city, I took a day to visit St. Cloud, and refresh myself by a glimpse of the imperial park there, and a little of Nature's privacy, if such could be had, which proved to be the case, for a more agreeable day I have rarely passed. The park, toward which I at once made my way, is an immense natural forest, sweeping up over gentle hills from the banks of the Seine, and brought into order and perspective by a system of carriageways and avenues, which radiate from nu-

merous centres like the boulevards of Paris. At these centres were fountains and statues, with sunlight falling upon them; and, looking along the cool, dusky avenues, as they opened, this way and that, upon these marble tableaux, the effect was very striking, and was not at all marred to my eye by the neglect into which the place had evidently fallen. The woods were just mellowing into October; the large, shining horse-chestnuts dropped at my feet as I walked along; the jay screamed over the trees; and occasionally a red squirrel — larger and softer-looking than ours, not so sleek, nor so noisy and vivacious — skipped among the branches. Soldiers passed, here and there, to and from some encampment on the farther side of the park; and, hidden from view somewhere in the forest-glades, a band of buglers filled the woods with wild musical strains.

English royal parks and pleasure grounds are quite different. There the prevailing character is pastoral,— immense stretches of lawn, dotted with the royal oak, and alive with deer. But the Frenchman loves forests evidently, and nearly all his pleasure grounds about Paris are immense woods. The Bois de Boulogne, the forests of Vincennes, of St. Germain, of Bondy, and I don't know how many others, are near at hand, and are much prized. What the animus of this love may be is not so clear. It cannot be a love of solitude, for the French are characteristically a social and gregarious people. It cannot be the English poetical or Words-

worthian feeling for Nature, because French literature does not show this sense or this kind of perception. I am inclined to think the forest is congenial to their love of form and their sharp perceptions, but more especially to that kind of fear and wildness which they at times exhibit; for civilization has not quenched the primitive ardor and fierceness of the Frenchman yet, and it is to be hoped it never may. He is still more than half a wild man, and, if turned loose in the woods, I think would develop, in tooth and nail, and in all the savage, brute instincts, more rapidly than the men of any other race, except possibly the Slavic. Have not his descendants in this country — the Canadian French — turned and lived with the Indians, and taken to wild, savage customs with more relish and genius than have any other people 1 How hairy and vehement and pantomimic he is! How his eyes glance from under his heavy brows! His type among the animals is the wolf, and one readily recalls how largely the wolf figures in the traditions and legends and folk-lore of Continental Europe, and how closely his remains are associated with those of man in the bone-caves of the geologists. He has not stalked through their forests and fascinated their imaginations so long for nothing. The she-wolf suckled other founders beside those of Eome. Especially when I read of the adventures of Eussian and Polish exiles in Siberia — men of aristocratic lineage wandering amid snow and arctic cold, sleeping in rocks or in hollow trees, and holding their own, empty-

handed, against hunger and frost and their fiercei brute embodiments — do I recognize a hardihood and a ferity whose wet-nurse, ages back, may well have been this gray slut of the woods.

It is this fierce, untamable core that gives the point and the splendid audacity to Erench literature and art, — its vehemence and impatience of restraint. It is the salt of their speech, the nitre of their wit. When morbid, it gives that rabid and epileptic tendency which sometimes shows itself in Victor Hugo. In this great writer, however, it more frequently takes the form of an aboriginal fierceness and hunger that glares and bristles, and is insatiable and omnivorous.

And how many times has Paris, that boudoir of beauty and fashion, proved to be a wolf's lair, swarming with jaws athirst for human throats! — the lust for blood and the greed for plunder, sleeping, biding their time, never extinguished.

I do not contemn it. To the natural historian it is good. It is a return to first principles again after so much art, and culture, and lying, and ehau-vinis7iie, and shows these old civilizations in no danger of becoming efi"ete yet. It is like the hell of fire beneath our feet, which the geologists tell us is the life of the globe. Were it not for it, who would not at times despair of the French character? As long as this fiery core remains, I shall believe France capable of recovering from any disaster to her arms. The "mortal ripening" of the nation is stayed.

The English and Germans, on the other hand, are saved by great breadth and heartiness, and a constitutional tendency to coarseness of fibre which art and civilization abate very little. What is to save us in this country, I wonder, who have not the French regnancy and fire, nor the Teutonic heartiness and vis inerticef and who are already in danger of refining or attenuating into a high-heeled, short-jawed, genteel race, with more brains than stomach, and more address than character ?

IV

FROM LONDON TO NEW YORK

I HAD imagined that the next best thing to see-ing England would be to see Scotland; but, as this latter pleasure was denied me, certainly the next best thing was seeing Scotland's greatest son. Carlyle has been so constantly and perhaps justly represented as a stormy and wrathful person, brewing bitter denunciation for America and Americans, that I cannot forbear to mention the sweet and genial mood in which we found him, — a gentle and affectionate grandfather, with his delicious Scotch brogue and rich, melodious talk, overflowing with reminiscences of his earlier life, of Scott and Goethe and Edinburgh, and other men and places he had known. Learning I was especially interested in birds, he discoursed of the lark and nightingale and mavis, framing his remarks about them in some episode of his personal experience, and investing their songs with the double charm of his description and his adventure.

"It is only geese who get plucked there," said my companion after we had left, — a man who had known Carlyle intimately for many years; "silly persons who have no veneration for the great man, and come to convert him or change his convictions

upon subjects to which he has devoted a lifetime of profound thought and meditation. With such persons he has no patience."

. Carlyle had just returned from Scotland, where he had spent the summer. The Scotch hills and mountains, he said, had an ancient, mournful look, as if the weight of immeasurable time had settled down upon them. Their look was in Ossian, — his spirit reflected theirs; and as I gazed upon the venerable man before me, and noted his homely and rugged yet profound and melancholy expression, I knew that their look was upon him also, and that a greater than Ossian had been nursed amid those lonely hills. Few men in literature have felt the burden of the world, the weight of the inexorable conscience, as has Carlyle, or drawn such fresh inspiration from that source. However we may differ from him (and almost in self-defense one must differ from a man of such intense and overweening personality), it must yet be admitted that he habitually speaks out of that primitive silence and solitude in which only the heroic soul dwells. Certainly not in contemporary British literature is there another writer whose bowstring has such a twang.

I left London in the early part of November, and turned my face westward, going leisurely through England and Wales, and stringing upon my thread a few of the famous places, as Oxford, Stratford, Warwick, Birmingham, Chester, and taking a last look of the benign land. The weather was fair; I was yoked to no companion, and was apparently the

only tourist on that route. The field occupations drew my eye as usual. They were very simple, and consisted mainly of the gathering of root crops. I saw no building of fences, or of houses or barns, and no draining or improving of any kind worth mentioning, these things having all been done long ago. Speaking of barns reminds me that I do not remember to have seen a building of this kind while in England, much less a group or cluster of them as at home; hay and grain being always stacked, and the mildness of the climate rendering a protection of this kind unnecessary for the cattle and sheep. In contrast, America may be called the country of barns and outbuildings: —

" Thou lucky Mistress of the tranquil barns," as Walt Whitman apostrophizes the Union.

I missed also many familiar features in the autumn fields, — those given to our landscape by Indian corn, for instance, the tent-like stouts, the shucks, the rustling blades, the ripe pumpkins strewing the field; for, notwithstanding England is such a garden, our corn does not flourish there. I saw no buckwheat either, the red stubble and little squat figures of the upright sheaves of which are so noticeable in our farming districts at this season. Neither did I see any gathering of apples, or orchards from which to gather them. "As sure as there are apples in Herefordshire " seems to be a proverb in England; yet it is very certain that the orchard is not the institution anywhere in Britain ,that it is in this country, or so prominent a feature in the landscape.

The native apples are inferior in size and quality, and are sold by the pound. Pears were more abundant at the fruit stands, and were of superior excellence and very cheap.

I hope it will not be set down to any egotism of my own, but rather to the effect upon an ardent pilgrim of the associations of the place and its renown in literature, that all my experience at Stratford seems worthy of recording, and to be invested with a sort of poetical interest, — even the fact that I walked up from the station with a handsome young countrywoman who had chanced to occupy a seat in the same compartment of the car with me from Warwick, and who, learning the nature of my visit, volunteered to show me the Eed Horse Inn, as her course led her that way. We walked mostly in the middle of the street, with our umbrellas hoisted, for it was raining slightly, while a boy whom we found lying in wait for such a chance trudged along in advance of us with my luggage.

At the Eed Horse the pilgrim is in no danger of having the charm and the poetical atmosphere with which he has surrounded himself dispelled, but rather enhanced and deepened, especially if he has the luck I had, to find few other guests, and to fall into the hands of one of those simple, strawberry-like English housemaids, who gives him a cosy, snug little parlor all to himself, as was the luck of Irving also; who answers his every summons, and looks into his eyes with the simplicity and directness of a child; who could step from no page but

that of Scott or the divine William himself; who puts the " coals " on your grate with her own hands, and, when you ask for a lunch, spreads the cloth on one end of the table while you sit reading or writing at the other, and places before you a whole haunch of delicious cold mutton, with bread and home-brewed ale, and requests you to help yourself; who, when bedtime arrives, lights you up to a clean, sweet chamber, with a high-canopied bed hung with snow-white curtains; who calls you in the morning, and makes ready your breakfast while you sit with your feet on the fender before the blazing grate; and to whom you pay your reckoning on leaving, having escaped entirely all the barrenness and publicity of hotel life, and had all the privacy and quiet of home without any of its cares or interruptions. And this, let me say here, is the great charm of the characteristic English inn; it has a domestic, homelike air. " Taking mine ease at mine inn " has a real significance in England. You can take your ease and more; you can take real solid comfort. In the first place, there is no barroom, and consequently no loafers or pimps, or fumes of tobacco or whiskey; then there is no landlord or proprietor or hotel clerk to lord it over you. The host, if there is such a person, has a way of keeping himself in the background, or absolutely out of sight, that is entirely admirable. You are monarch of all you survey. You are not made to feel that it is in some one else's house you are stopping, and that you must court the master for his favor. It is your

house, you are the master, and you have only to enjoy your own.

In the gray, misty afternoon, I walked out over the Avon, like all English streams full to its grassy brim, and its current betrayed only by a floating leaf or feather, and along English fields and roads, and noted the familiar sights and sounds and smells of autumn. The spire of the church where Shakespeare lies buried shot up stately and tall from the banks of the Avon, a little removed from the village; and the church itself, more like a cathedral in size and beauty, was also visible above the trees. Thitherward I soon bent my steps, and while I was lingering among the graves, ^ reading the names and dates so many centuries old, and surveying the gray and weather-worn exterior of the church, the slow tolling of the bell announced a funeral. Upon such a stage, and amid such surroundings, with all this past for a background, the shadowy figure of the peerless bard towering over all, the incident of the moment had a strange interest to me, and I looked about for the funeral cortege. Presently a group of three or four figures appeared at the head of the avenue of limes, the foremost of them a woman, bearing an infant's coffin under her arm, wrapped in a white sheet. The clerk and sexton, with their robes on, went out to meet them, and conducted them into the church, where the service proper to

1 In England the chnrch always stands in the midst of the graveyard, and hence can be approached only on foot. People, it seems, never go to church in carriages or wagons, but on foot, along paths and lanes.

such occasions was read, after which the coffin was taken out as it was brought in, and lowered into the grave. It was the smallest funeral I ever saw, and my efforts to play the part of a sympathizing public by hovering in the background, I fear, was only an intrusion after all.

Having loitered to my heart's content amid the stillness of the old church, and paced to and fro above the illustrious dead, I set out, with the sun about an hour high, to see the house of Anne Hathaway at Shottery, shunning the highway and following a path that followed hedge-rows, crossed meadows and pastures, skirted turnip fields and cabbage patches, to a quaint gathering of low thatched houses, — a little village of farmers and laborers, about a mile from Stratford. At the gate in front of the house a boy was hitching a little gray donkey, almost hidden beneath two immense panniers filled with coarse hay.

" Whose house is this 1 " inquired I, not being quite able to make out the name.

"Hann' Ataway's 'ouse," said he.

So I took a good look at Anne's house, — a homely, human-looking habitation, with its old oak beams and thatched roof, — but did not go in, as Mrs. Baker, who was eying me from the door, evidently hoped I would, but chose rather to walk past it and up the slight rise of ground beyond, where I paused and looked out over the fields, just lit up by the setting sun. Returning, I stepped into the Shakespeare Tavern, a little, homely wayside place

or more like a path, apart from the main road, and the good dame brought me some "home-brewed," which I drank sitting by a rude table on a rude bench in a small, low room, with a stone floor and an immense chimney. The coals burned cheerily, and the crane and hooks in the fireplace called up visions of my earliest childhood. Apparently the house and the surroundings, and the atmosphere of the place and the ways of the people, were what they were three hundred years ago. It was all sweet and good, and I enjoyed it hugely, and was much refreshed.

Crossing the fields in the gloaming, I came up with some children, each with a tin bucket of milk, threading their way toward Stratford. The little girl, a child ten years old, having a larger bucket than the rest, was obliged to set down her burden every few rods and rest; so I lent her a helping hand. I thought her prattle, in that broad but musical patois, and along these old hedge-rows, the most delicious I ever heard. She said they came to Shottery for milk because it was much better than they got at Stratford. In America they had a cow of their own. Had she lived in America, then ? " Oh, yes, four years, '^ and the stream of her talk was fuller at once. But I hardly recognized even the name of my own country in her innocent prattle; it seemed like a land of fable, —all had a remote mythological air, and I pressed my inquiries as if I was hearing of this strange land for the first time. She had an uncle still living in the " States

of Hoio," but exactly where her father had lived was not so clear. In The States somewhere, and in "Ogden's Valley." There was a lake there that had salt in it, and not far off was the sea. "In America," she said, and she gave such a sweet and novel twang to her words, "we had a cow of our own, and two horses and a wagon and a dog." "Yes," joined in her little brother, "and nice chickens and a goose." "But," continued the sister, "we owns none o' them here. In America 'most everybody owned their houses, and we could a' owned a house if we had stayid."

" What made you leave America ? " I inquired.

"'Cause me father wanted to see his friends."

"Did your mother want to come back?"

"No, me mother wanted to stay in America."

"Is food as plenty here, —do you have as much to eat as in The States ?"

" Oh, yes, and more. The first year we were in America we could not get enough to eat."

"But you do not get meat very often here, do you?"

"Quite often," — not so confidently.

"How often?"

"Well, sometimes we has pig's liver in the week time, and we allers has meat of a Sunday; we likes meat."

Here we emerged from the fields into the highway, and the happy children went their way and I mine.

In the evening, as I was strolling about the town,

a poor, crippled,, half-witted fellow came jerking himself across the street after me and offered himself as a guide.

"I'm the feller what showed Artemus Ward around when he was here. You 've heerd on me, I expect? Not? Why, he characterized me in Punch,' he did. He asked me if Shakespeare took all the wit out of Stratford ? And this is what I said to him: * No, he left some for me.' "

But not wishing to be guided just then, I bought the poor fellow off with a few pence, and kept on my way.

Stratford is a quiet old place, and seems mainly the abode of simple common folk. One sees no marked signs of either poverty or riches. It is situated in a beautiful expanse of rich, rolling farming country, but bears little resemblance to a rural town in America: not a tree, not a spear of grass; the houses packed close together and crowded up on the street, the older ones presenting their gables and showing their structure of oak beams. English oak seems incapable of decay even when exposed to the weather, while indoors it takes three or four centuries to give it its best polish and hue.

I took my last view of Stratford quite early of a bright Sunday morning, when the ground was white with a dense hoar-frost. The great church, as I approached it, loomed up under the sun through a bank of blue mist. The Avon was like glass, with little wraiths of vapor clinging here and there to its surface. Two white swans stood on its banks in

front of the church, and, without regarding the mirror that so drew my eye, preened their plumage; while, farther up, a piebald cow reached down for some grass under the brink where the frost had not settled, and a piebald cow in the river reached up for the same morsel. Rooks and crows and jackdaws were noisy in the trees overhead and about the church spire. I stood a long while musing upon the scene.

At the birthplace of the poet, the keeper, an elderly woman, shivered with cold as she showed me about. The primitive, home-made appearance of things, the stone floor much worn and broken, the rude oak beams and doors, the leaden sash with the little window-panes scratched full of names, among others that of Walter Scott, the great chimneys where quite a family could literally sit in the chimney corner, etc., were what I expected to see, and looked very human and good. It is impossible to associate anything but sterling qualities and simple, healthful characters with these early English birthplaces. They are nests built with faithfulness and affection, and through them one seems to get a glimpse of devouter, sturdier times.

From Stratford I went back to Warwick, thence to Birmingham, thence to Shrewsbury, thence to Chester, the old Roman camp, thence to Holyhead, being intent on getting a glimpse of Wales and the Welsh, and maybe taking a tramp up Snowdon or some of his congeners, for my legs literally ached for a mountain climb, a certain set of muscles being

80 long unused. . In the course of my journeyings, I tried each class or compartment of the cars, first, second, and third, and found but little choice. The difference is simply in the upholstering, and, if you are provided with a good shawl or wrap-up, you need not be particular about that. In the first, the floor is carpeted and the seats substantially upholstered, usually in blue woolen cloth; in the second, the seat alone is cushioned; and in the third, you sit on a bare

bench. But all classes go by the same train, and often in the same car, or carriage, as they say here. In the first class, travel the real and the shoddy nobility and Americans; in the second, commercial and professional men; and in the third, the same, with such of the peasantry and humbler classes as travel by rail. The only annoyance I experienced in the third class arose from the freedom with which the smokers, always largely in the majority, indulged in their favorite pastime. (I perceive there is one advantage in being a smoker: you are never at a loss for something to do, — you can smoke.)

At Chester I stopped overnight, selecting my hotel for its name, the "Green Dragon." It was Sunday night, and the only street scene my rambles afforded was quite, a large gathering of persons on a corner, listening, apparently with indifference or curiosity, to an ignorant, hot-headed street preacher. "Now I am going to tell you something you will not like to hear, — 'something that will make you angry. I know it will. It is this: I expect to go

to heaven. I am perfectly confident I shall go there. I know you do not like that." But why his hearers should not like that did not appear. For my part, I thought, for the good of all concerned, the sooner he went the better.

In the morning, I mounted the wall in front of the cathedral, and, with a very lively feeling of wonder and astonishment, walked completely around the town on top of it, a distance of about two miles. The wall, being in places as high as the houses, afforded some interesting views into attics, chambers, back yards, etc. I envied the citizens such a delightful promenade ground, full of variety and interest. Just the right distance, too, for a brisk turn to get up an appetite, or a leisurely stroll to tone down a dinner; while as a place for chance meetings of happy lovers, or to get away from one's companions if the flame must burn in secret and in silence, it is unsurpassed. I occasionally met or passed other pedestrians, but noticed that it required a brisk pace to lessen the distance between myself and an attractive girlish figure a few hundred feet in advance of me. The railroad cuts across one corner of the town, piercing the walls with two very carefully constructed archways. Indeed, the people are very choice of the wall, and one sees posted notices of the city authorities offering a reward for any one detected in injuring it. It has stood now some seven or eight centuries, and from appearances is good for one or two more. There are several towers on the wall, from one of which some English king,

over two hundred years ago, witnessed the defeat of his army on Kowton Moor. But when I was there, though the sun was shining, the atmosphere was so loaded with smoke that I could not catch even a glimpse of the moor where the battle took place. There is a gateway through the wall on each of the four sides, and this slender and beautiful but blackened and worn span, as if to afford a transit from the chamber windows on one side of the street to those of the other, is the first glimpse the traveler gets of the wall. The gates beneath the arches have entirely disappeared. The ancient and carved oak fronts of the buildings on the main street, and the inclosed sidewalk that ran through the second stories of the shops and stores, were not less strange and novel to me. The sidewalk was like a gentle upheaval in its swervings and undulations, or like a walk through the woods, the oaken posts and braces on the outside answering for the trees, and the prospect ahead for the vista.

The ride along the coast of Wales was crowded with novelty and interest,— the sea on one side and the mountains on the other, — the latter bleak and heathery in the foreground, but cloud-capped and snow-white in the distance. The afternoon was dark and lowering, and just before entering Conway we had a very striking view. A turn in the road suddenly brought us to where we looked through a black framework of heathery hills, and beheld Snowdon and his chiefs apparently with the full rigors of winter upon them. It was so satisfying that I lost at once my desire to tramp up them. I barely had time to turn from the mountains to get a view of Conway Castle, one of the largest and most impressive ruins I saw. The train cuts close to the great round tower, and plunges through the wall of gray, shelving stone into the bluff beyond, giving the traveler only time to glance and marvel.

About the only glimpse I got of the Welsh character was on this route. At one of the stations, Abergele I think, a fresh, blooming young woman got into our compartment, occupied by myself and two commercial travelers (bag-men, or, as we say, " drummers "), and, before she could take her seat, was complimented by one of them on her good looks. Feeling in a measure responsible for the honor and good-breeding of the compartment, I could hardly conceal my embarrassment; but the young Abergeless herself did not seem to take it amiss, and, when presently the jolly bag-man addressed his conversation to her, replied beseemingly and good-naturedly. As she arose to leave the car at her destination, a few stations beyond, he said "he thought it a pity that such a sweet, pretty girl should leave us so soon," and seizing her hand the audacious rascal actually solicited a kiss. I expected this would be the one drop too much, and that we should have a scene, and began to regard myself in the light of an avenger of an insulted Welsh beauty, Avhen my heroine paused, and I believe actually deliberated whether or not to comply

before two spectators! Certain it is that she yielded the highwayman her hand, and, bidding him a gentle good-night in Welsh, smilingly and blush ingly left the car. "Ah," said the villain, "these Welsh girls are capital; I know them like a book, and have had many a lark with them."

At Holyhead I got another glimpse of the Welsh. I had booked for Dublin, and having several hours on my hands of a dark, threatening night before the departure of the steamer, I sallied out in the old town tilted up against the side of the hill, in the most adventurous spirit I could summon up, threading my way through the dark, deserted streets, pausing for a moment in front of a small house with closed doors and closely-shuttered windows, where I heard suppressed voices, the monotonous scraping of a fiddle, and a lively shuffling of feet, and passing on finally entered, drawn by the musical strains, a quaint old place, where a blind harper, seated in the corner of a rude kind of coffee and sitting room, was playing on a harp. I liked the atmosphere of the place, so primitive and wholesome, and was quite willing to have my attention drawn off from the increasing storm without, and from the bitter cup which I knew the Irish sea was preparing for me. The harper presently struck up a livelier strain, when two Welsh girls, who were chatting before the grate, one of them as dumpy as a bag of meal and the other slender and tall, stepped into the middle of the floor and began to dance to the delicious music, a Welsh mechanic and myself drink-

ing our ale and looking on approvingly. After a while the pleasant, modest-looking bar-maid, whom I had seen behind the beer-levers as I entered, came in, and, after looking on for a moment, was persuaded to lay down her sewing and join in the dance. Then there came in a sandy-haired Welshman, who could speak and understand only his native dialect, and finding his neighbors affiliating with an Englishman, as he supposed, and trying to speak the hateful tongue, proceeded to berate them sharply (for it appears the Welsh are still jealous of the English); but when they explained to him that I was not an Englishman, but an American, and had already twice stood the beer all around (at an outlay of sixpence), he subsided into a sulky silence, and regarded me intently.

About eleven o'clock a policeman paused at the door, and intimated that it was time the house was shut up and the music stopped, and to outward appearances his friendly warning was complied with; but the harp still discoursed in a minor key, and a light tripping and shuffling of responsive feet might occasionally have been heard for an hour later. When I arose to go, it was with a feeling of regret that I could not see more of this simple and social people, with whom I at once felt that "touch of nature" which "makes the whole world kin," and my leave-taking was warm and hearty accordingly.

Through the wind and the darkness I threaded my way to the wharf, and in less than two hours afterward was a most penitent voyager, and fitfully

joining in that doleful gastriloquial chorus that so often goes up from the cabins of those Channel steamers.

I hardly know why I went to Ireland, except it was to indulge the few drops of Irish bloo'd in my veins, and maybe also with a view to shorten my sea voyage by a day. I also felt a desire to see one or two literary men there, and in this sense my journey was eminently gratifying; but so far from shortening my voyage by a day, it lengthened it by three days, that being the time it took me to recover from the effects of it; and as to the tie of blood, I think it must nearly all have run out, for I felt but few congenital throbs while in Ireland.

The Englishman at home is a much more lovable animal than the Englishman abroad, but Pat in Ireland is even more of a pig than in this country. Indeed, the squalor and poverty, and cold, skinny wretchedness one sees in Ireland, and (what freezes our sympathies) the groveling, swiny shiftlessness that pervades these hovels, no traveler can be prepared for. It is the bare prose of misery, the un-heroic of tragedy. There is not one redeeming or mitigating feature.

E-ailway traveling in Ireland is not so rapid or so cheap as in England. Neither are the hotels as good or as clean, or the fields so well kept, or the look of the country so thrifty and peaceful. The dissatisfaction of the people is in the very air. Ireland looks sour and sad. She looks old, too, as do all those countries beyond seas,— old in a way that

the American is a stranger to. It is not the age of nature, the unshaken permanence of the hills through long periods of time, but the weight of human years and human sorrows, as if the earth sympathized with man and took on his attributes and infirmities.

I did not go much about Dublin, and the most characteristic thing I saw there were those queer, uncomfortable dog-carts, — a sort of Irish bull on wheels, with the driver on one side balancing the passenger on the other, and the luggage occupying the seat of safety between. It comes the nearest to riding on horseback, and on a side-saddle at that, of any vehicle-traveling I ever did.

I stopped part of a day at Mallow, an old town on the Blackwater, in one of the most fertile agricultural districts of Ireland. The situation is fine, and an American naturally expects to see a charming rural town, planted with trees and filled with clean, comfortable homes; but he finds instead a wretched place, smitten with a plague of filth and mud, and offering but one object upon which the eye can dwell with pleasure, and that is the ruins of an old castle, "Mallow Castle over Blackwater," which dates back to the time of Queen Elizabeth. It stands amid noble trees on the banks of the river, and its walls, some of them thirty or forty feet high, are completely overrun with ivy. The Black-water, a rapid, amber-colored stream, is spanned at this point by a superb granite bridge.

And I will say here that anything like a rural

town in our sense, — a town with trees and grass and large spaces about the houses, gardens, yards, shrubbery, coolness, fragrance, etc., — seems unknown in England or Ireland. The towns and villages are all remnants of feudal times, and seem to have been built with an eye to safety and compactness, or else IT 2X1 were more social, and loved to get closer together, then than now. Perhaps the. damp, chilly climate made them draw nearer together. At any rate, the country towns are little cities; or rather it is as if another London had been cut up in little and big pieces and distributed over the land.

In the afternoon, to take the kinks out of my legs, and quicken, if possible, my circulation a little, which since the passage over the Channel had felt as if it was thick and green, I walked rapidly to the top of the Kockmeledown Mountains, getting a good view of Irish fields and roads and fences as I went up, and a very wide and extensive view of the country after I had reached the summit, and improving the atmosphere of my physical tenement amazingly. These mountains have no trees' or bushes or other growth than a harsh prickly heather, about a foot high, which begins exactly at the foot of the mountain. You are walking on smooth, fine meadow land, when you leap a fence and there is the heather. On the highest point of this mountain, and on the highest point of all the mountains around, was a low stone mound, which I was puzzled to know the meaning of. Standing there, the country rolled away beneath me under a cold, gray November sky, and, as was the case with the English landscape, looked singularly desolate,— the desolation of a dearth of human homes, industrial centres, families, workers, and owners of the soil. Few roads, scarce ever a vehicle, no barns, no groups of bright, well-ordered buildings, indeed no farms and neighborhoods and schoolhouses, but a wide spread of rich, highly cultivated country, with here and there, visible to close scrutiny, small gray stone houses with thatched roofs, the abodes of poverty and wretchedness. A recent English writer says the first thing that struck him in American landscape-painting was the absence of man and the domestic animals from the pictures, and the preponderance of rude, wild nature; and his first view of this country seems to have made the same impression. But it is certainly true that the traveler through any of our older States will see ten houses, rural habitations, to one in England or Ireland, though, as a matter of course, nature here looks much less domesticated, and much less expressive of human occupancy and contact. The Old World people have clung to the soil closer and more lovingly than we do. The ground has been more precious. They have had none to waste, and have made the most of every inch of it. "Wherever they have touched they have taken root and thriven as best they could. Then the American is more cosmopolitan and less domestic. He is not so local in his feelings and attachments. He does not bestow himself upon the earth or upon his home as his ancestors did. He feathers his nest very little. Why should he ? He may migrate to-morrow and build another. He is like the passenger pigeon that lays its eggs and rears its young upon a little platform of bare twigs. Our poverty and nakedness is in this respect, I think, beyond dispute. There is nothing nest-like about our homes, either in their interiors or exteriors. Even wealth and taste and foreign aids rarely attain that cosy, mellowing atmosphere that pervades not only the lowly birthplaces but the halls and manor houses of older lands. And what do our farms represent but so much real estate, so much cash value ?

Only where man loves the soil, and nestles to it closely and long, will it take on this beneficent and human look which foreign travelers miss in our landscape; and only where homes are built with fondness and emotion, and in obedience to the social, paternal, and domestic instincts, will they hold the charm and radiate and be warm with the feeling I have described.

And, while I am upon the subject, I will add that European cities differ from ours in this same particular. They have a homelier character, —more the air of dwelling-places, the abodes of men drawn together for other purposes than traffic. People actually live in them, and find life sweet and festal. But what does our greatest city. New York, express besides commerce or politics, or what other reason has it for its existence? This is, of course, in a measure the result of the modern worldly and practical business spirit which more and more animates

all nations, and which led Carlyle to say of his own countrymen that they were becoming daily more "flat, stupid, and mammonish." Yet I am persuaded that in our case it is traceable also to the leanness and depletion of our social and convivial instincts, and to the fact that the material cares of life are more serious and engrossing with us than with any other people.

I spent part of a day at Cork, wandering about the town, threading my way through the back streets and alleys, and seeing life reduced to fewer makeshifts than I had ever before dreamed of. I went through, or rather skirted, a kind of secondhand market, where the most sorry and dilapidated articles of clothing and household utensils were offered for sale, and where the cobblers were cobbling up old shoes that would hardly hold together. Then the wretched old women one sees, without any sprinkling of young ones,— youth and age alike bloomless and unlovely.

In a meadow on the hills that encompass the city, I found the American dandelion in bloom, and some large red clover, and started up some skylarks as I might start up the field sparrows in our own up-lying fields.

Is the magpie a Celt and a Catholic 1 1 saw not one in England, but plenty of them in France, and again when I reached Ireland.

At Queenstown I awaited the steamer from Liverpool, and about nine o'clock in the morning was delighted to see her long black form moving up the

bay. She came to anchor about a mile or two out, and a little tug was in readiness to take us off. A score or more of emigrants, each with a bag and box, had been waiting all the morning at the wharf. When the time of embarkation arrived, the agent stepped aboard the tug and called out their names one by one, when Bridget and Catherine and Patrick and Michael, and the rest, came aboard, received their tickets, and passed "forward," with a half-frightened, half-bewildered look. But not much emotion was displayed until the boat began to move off, when the tears fell freely, and they continued to fall faster and faster, and the sobs to come thicker and thicker, until, as the faces of friends began to fade on the wharf, both men and women burst out into a loud, unrestrained bawl. This sudden demonstration of grief seemed to frighten the children and smaller fry, who up to this time had been very jovial; but now, suspecting something was Avrong, they all broke out in a most pitiful chorus, forming an anti-climax to the wail of their parents that was quite amusing, and that seemed to have its effect upon the "children of a larger growth," for they instantly hushed their lamentations and turned their attention toward the great steamer. There was a rugged but bewildered old granny among them, on her way to join her daughter somewhere in the interior of New York, who seemed to regard me with a kindred eye, and toward whom, I confess, I felt some family affinity. Before we had got half way to the vessel, the dear old creature missed a sheet from

her precious bundle of worldly effects, and very confidentially told me that her suspicions pointed to the stoker, a bristling, sooty "wild Irishman." The stoker resented the insinuation, and I overheard him berating the old lady in Irish so sharply and threateningly (I had no doubt of his guilt) that she was quite frightened, and ready to retract the charge to hush the man up. She seemed to think her troubles had just begun. If they behaved thus to her on the little tug, what would they not do on board the great black steamer itself? So when she got separated from her luggage in getting aboard the vessel, her excitement was great, and I met her following about the man whom she had accused of filching her bed linen, as if he must have the clew to the lost bed itself. Her face brightened when she saw me, and, giving me a terribly hard wink and a most expressive nudge, said she wished I would keep near her a little. This I did, and soon had the pleasure of leaving her happy and reassured beside her box and bundle.

The passage home, though a rough one, was cheerfully and patiently borne. I found a compound motion, — the motion of a screw steamer, a roll and a plunge — less trying to my head than the simple rocking or pitching of the side-wheeled Scotia. One motion was in a measure a foil to the other. My brain, acted upon by two forces, was compelled to take the hypothenuse, and I think the concussion was considerably diminished thereby. The vessel was forever trembling upon the verge of immense

watery chasms that opened now under her port bows, now under her starboard, and that ahnost made one catch for his breath as he looked into them; yet the noble ship had a way of skirting them or striding across them that was quite wonderful. Only five days was I compelled to " hole up " in my stateroom, hibernating, weathering the final rude shock of the Atlantic. Part of this time I was capable of feeling a languid interest in the oscillations of my coat suspended from a hook in the door. Back and forth, back and forth, all day long, vibrated this black pendulum, at long intervals touching the sides of the room, indicating great lateral or diagonal motion of the ship. The great waves, I observed, go in packs like wolves. Now one would pounce upon her, then another, then another, in quick succession, making the ship strain every nerve to shake them off. Then she would glide along quietly for some minutes, and my coat would register but a few degrees in its imaginary arc, when another band of the careering demons would cross our path and harass us as before. Sometimes they would pound and thump on the sides of the vessel like immense sledge-hammers, beginning away up toward the bows and quickly running down her whole length, jarring, raking, and venting their wrath in a very audible manner; or a wave would rake along the side with a sharp, ringing, metallic sound, like a huge spear-point seeking a vulnerable place; or some hard-backed monster would rise up from the deep and grate and bump the whole length

of the keel, forcibly suggesting hidden rocks and consequent wreck and ruin.

Then it seems there is always some biggest wave to be met with somewhere on the voyage,— a monster billow that engulfs disabled vessels, and sometimes carries away parts of the rigging of the stanch-est. This big wave struck us the third day out about midnight, and nearly threw us all out of our berths, and careened the ship over so far that it seemed to take her last pound of strength to right herself up again. There was a slamming of doors, a rush of crockery, and a screaming of women, heard above the general din and confusion, while the steerage passengers thought their last hour had come. The vessel before us encountered this giant wave during a storm in mid-ocean, and was completely buried beneath it; one of the officers was swept overboard, the engines suddenly stopped, and there was a terrible moment during which it seemed uncertain whether the vessel would shake off the sea or go to the bottom.

Besides observing the oscillations of my coat, I had at times a stupid satisfaction in seeing my two new London trunks belabor each other about my stateroom floor. Nearly every day they would break from their fastenings under my berth and start on a wild race for the opposite side of the room. Naturally enough, the little trunk would always get the start of the big one, but the big one followed close, and sometimes caught the little one in a very uncomfortable manner. Once a knife and

fork and a breakfast plate slipped off the sofa and joined in the race; but, if not distanced, they got sadly the worst of it, especially the plate. But the carpet had the most reason to complain. Two or three turns sufficed to loosen it from the floor, when, shoved to one side, the two trunks took turns in butting it. I used to allow this sport to go on till it grew monotonous, when I would alternately shout and ring until "Eobert" appeared and restored order.

The condition of certain picture-frames and vases and other frail articles among my effects, when I reached home, called to mind not very pleasantly this trunken frolic.

It is impossible not to sympathize with the ship in her struggles with the waves. You are lying there wedged into your berth, and she seems indeed a thing of life and conscious power. She is built entirely of iron, is 500 feet long, and, besides other freight, carries 2,500 tons of railroad iron, which lies down there flat in her bottom, a dead, indigestible weight, so unlike a cargo in bulk, yet she is a quickened spirit for all that. You feel every wave that strikes her; you feel the sea bearing her down; she has run her nose into one of those huge swells, and a solid blue wall of water tons in weight comes over her bows and floods her forward deck; she braces herself, every rod and rivet and timber seems to lend its support; you almost expect to see the wooden walls of your room grow rigid with muscular contraction; she trembles from stem to stern, she recovers, she breaks the gripe of her antagonist, and, rising up, shakes the sea from her with a kind of gleeful wrath; I hear the torrents of water rush along the lower decks, and, finding a means of escape, pour back into the sea, glad to get away on any terms, and I say, "Noble ship! you are indeed a god! "

I wanted to see a first-class storm at sea, and perhaps ought to be satisfied with the heavy blow or hurricane we had when off Sable Island, but I confess I was not, though, by the lying-to of the vessel and the frequent soundings, it was evident there was danger about. A dense fog uprose, which did not drift like a land fog, but was as immovable as iron; it was like a spell, a misty enchantment; and out of this fog came the wind, a steady, booming blast, that smote the ship over on her side and held her there, and howled in the rigging like a chorus of fiends. The waves did not know which way to flee; they were heaped up and then scattered in a twinkling. I thought of the terrible line of one of our poets: —

" The spasm of the sky and the shatter of the sea." The sea looked wrinkled and old and oh, so pitiless! I had stood long before Turner's "Shipwreck" in the National Gallery in London, and this sea recalled his, and I appreciated more than ever the artist's great powers.

These storms, it appears, are rotary in their wild dance and promenade up and down the seas. "Look the wind squarely in the teeth," said an ex-sea-captain among the passengers, "and eight points to the right in the northern hemisphere will be the centre of the storm, and eight points to the left in the southern hemisphere."' I remembered that, in Victor Hugo's terrible dynamics, storms revolved in the other direction in the northern hemisphere, or followed the hands of a watch, while south of the equator they no doubt have ways equally original.

Late in the afternoon the storm abated, the fog was suddenly laid, and, looking toward the setting sun, I saw him athwart the wildest, most desolate scene in which it was ever my fortune to behold the face of that god. The sea was terribly agitated, and the endless succession of leaping, frothing waves between me and the glowing west formed a picture I shall not soon forget.

I think the excuse that is often made in behalf of American literature, namely, that our people are too busy with other things yet, and will show the proper aptitude in this field, too, as soon as leisure is afforded, is fully justified by events of daily occurrence. Throw a number of them together without anything else to do, and they at once communicate to each other the itch of authorship. Confine them on board an ocean steamer, and by the third or fourth day a large number of them will break out all over with a sort of literary rash that nothing will assuage but some newspaper or journalistic enterprise which will give the poems and essays and jokes with which they are surcharged a chance to be seen and heard of men. I doubt if the like evei occurs among travelers of any other nationality. Englishmen or Frenchmen or Germans want something more warm and human, if less "refined;" but the average American, when in company, likes nothing so well as an opportunity to show the national trait of "smartness." There is not a bit of danger that we shall ever relapse into barbarism while so much latent literature lies at the bottom of our daily cares and advocations, and is sure to come to the surface the monient the latter are suspended or annulled!

While abreast of New England, and I don't know how many miles at sea, as I turned in my deck promenade, I distinctly scented the land,— a subtle, delicious odor of farms and homesteads, warm and human, that floated on the wild sea air, a promise and a token. The broad red line that had been slowly creeping across our chart for so many weary days, indicating the path of the ship, had now completely bridged the chasm, and had got a good purchase down under the southern coast of New England, and according to the reckoning we ought to have made Sandy Hook that night; but though the position of the vessel was no doubt theoretically all right, yet practically she proved to be much farther out at sea, for all that afternoon and night she held steadily on her course, and not till next morning did the coast of Long Island, like a thin, broken cloud just defined on the horizon, come into view. But before many hours we had

passed the Hook, and were moving slowly up the bay in the midday splendor of the powerful and dazzling light of the New World sun. And how good things looked to me after even so brief an absence! — the brilliancy, the roominess, the deep transparent blue of the sky, the clear, sharp outlines, the metropolitan splendor of New York, and especially of Broadway; and as I walked up that great thoroughfare, and noted the familiar physiognomy and the native nonchalance and independence, I experienced the delight that only the returned traveler can feel,—the instant preference of one's own country and countrymen over all the rest of the world.

THE END

Printed in Great Britain
by Amazon

37618591R00053

NATURE

MYSTICISM

(1913)

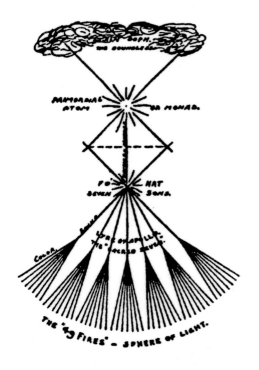

DESCENT OF SPIRIT INTO MATTER.

"All Things From One."

J. Edward Mercer